If Anything Should Happen...

by

Jennifer Ditri Frangella

The contents of this work, including, but not limited to, the accuracy of events, people, and places depicted; opinions expressed; permission to use previously published materials included; and any advice given or actions advocated are solely the responsibility of the author, who assumes all liability for said work and indemnifies the publisher against any claims stemming from publication of the work.

All Rights Reserved
Copyright © 2021 by Jennifer Ditri Frangella

No part of this book may be reproduced or transmitted, downloaded, distributed, reverse engineered, or stored in or introduced into any information storage and retrieval system, in any form or by any means, including photocopying and recording, whether electronic or mechanical, now known or hereinafter invented without permission in writing from the publisher.

Dorrance Publishing Co
585 Alpha Drive
Pittsburgh, PA 15238
Visit our website at *www.dorrancebookstore.com*

ISBN: 978-1-6386-7046-9
eISBN: 978-1-6386-7994-3

DAY 1

Chapter 1

Now – How I Got Here

Alcohol is such a fickle bitch; one minute I'm enjoying a nice bottle of rosé and some vodka shots, then the next minute I'm filling out a registration form and making an electronic payment to Marie Wilson, Ph.D. It only took one drunken click on the link in an email from Luci to send me on this journey through my own personal hell. I am locked in for four days at a grief retreat with a bunch of strangers. I've been running away from my memories for eight years (and doing a pretty good job of it, too) - the thought of being shackled to them for four days with people I don't know, feeling sorry for me, is the last thing I want. Luci is the one person in my life who has been by my side without fail, and it turns out she's sick of my shit. She dropped me here with a duffle bag full of wrinkled clothes and a toothbrush (…and a fifth of Fireball she doesn't know about). She has promised to return for me at the end of this retreat, unless I run out of this place screaming before time is up. Luci has assured me that if I do go AWOL, then I'll be placing an ad for a new roomie (and new bestie). It may sound like a harsh ultimatum, but if you knew how bad my behavior has been, then you'd see I deserve it.

Chapter 2

Last Month - The Ultimatum

When Luci tells me to get my head out of my ass, I know I've crossed a line. She has been with me through years of joy, helped me through years filled with grief and tragedy, and tolerated my years of anger and self-destruction. I know it hasn't been easy to be my friend, and it has recently become apparent that Luci isn't up for the "How-drunk-will-Silvia-be-when-she-comes-home-and-will-she-bring-a-random-guy-with-her?" game anymore. Our relationship has been quietly suffering for months, probably years. For the last several years, I've been living a very…how shall I put it. Controversial lifestyle? I tend to be introverted until you get a little booze or pot in me and then I'm my own private version of "Girls Gone Wild." After a particularly rowdy night involving a bottle of vodka, a dime bag of purple bud, and a delightfully fit doorman from the bar where I work, Luci put her foot down.

"*Morning!*" *Luci called a little too loudly as she kicked a blanket over the perfect, naked ass of whatever his name was lying next to me.*

"Mlugh." *It's all I could spit out.*

"*We need to talk.*" *Luci jiggled my leg with her foot, trying to rouse me from the warmth and comfort of my bed.*

"Coffee, pleeeaaase. I think I'm dying." *My head was pounding, and my mouth felt like a kitten and a turd had a baby on my tongue.*

After some more prodding, I begrudgingly rolled out of my cozy cocoon and followed Luci to our tiny kitchen. She poured water into the coffee maker and added the grounds. She was silent as the coffee brewed and my stomach was churning. Hangover? Anticipation of what Luci wanted to discuss? Probably both. The coffee maker made its gurgle-y water noises, and in minutes, I had my hands wrapped around an oversized mug and was sipping the warm, soothing elixir. Luci's new boyfriend walked out of her bedroom, gave me a tight, closed-lip smile, grabbed a cup of coffee, and headed to the living room. I felt an air of judgment coming from him, but it could've been my imagination.

"So who's the guy this time?" Luci asked in a clipped tone. I shrugged and rolled my eyes. Luci stepped toward me and took me by the shoulders, looked me in the eyes and asked, "Are you still in there, Silvia? I'm having a hard time finding you. You're out of control, and I'm sick of worrying about you all of the time. I'm scared that one morning you'll wake up and you'll be all the way gone. Your body will be here, but every last drop of the person I know and love will be gone. I know you think you're fine, but you're not. You're not living, not really. You've been trying to hide yourself in a bottle of booze or in some guy's, any guy's, bed. It's disgraceful. I don't even feel sorry for you anymore, I just feel…sick. I'm not trying to mom you, but girl, I can't do this anymore."

She was talking fast, like she was trying to beat the clock on a game show. I tried to take in what she was saying to me, but my brain was under a thick layer of hangover fog, and words weren't properly forming into sentences, so I sat there – staring at her.

My face must have looked as dumb as my mind felt because she looked at me and scoffed, "Am I boring you, Silvia? You know what? Go back to bed. I knew this was a bad idea. You aren't listening."

I know I must have really pissed her off. Her anger felt different this time, like she was waving a white flag and completely giving up on me, like she doesn't think I'm worth her effort anymore. I felt panicked on the inside, but my facial expressions were not cooperating with me.

I yelled out a little too loudly, "I'm sorry, Luci. I'm trying. Just…I'm still trying to wake up…"

Luci turned on me and yelled, her eyes smoldering with anger, "No! You aren't trying! That's the point. You're stuck and you're constantly re-living that night and then getting fucked up to make it go away. Callie died, not you!" Luci almost never yelled – it was part of the rules her dad gave her when she was little, to avoid having other kids fear her when she was the only black student in our very white school. Old habits die hard. Then more quietly she said, "I loved Callie, too, she wasn't my sister, but I loved her like one. It was *horrible when she died, but this is worse. It's like I'm watching you slowly die."* She wasn't wrong - I am absolutely guilty. I have made my life very small; it consists of Luci, my crappy bar job, alcohol, and pot…and that's about it. I hang out with a few of the people at the bar where I work every now and again, but I don't really fully connect with any of them. We drink together and hang out after the closing shift sometimes. I occasionally (okay, more than occasionally) bring one of them home for the night, but that's it. Other than that, I have a nice, friendly relationship with my Door Dash delivery guy, Paul, but I don't think I can count him as a friend. *"Here."* She handed me a paper that she seemed to produce out of thin air. *"I sent you an email, too. It should have a link to click, so you can register. I can't force you to go, Sil, but I can't watch you hurt yourself anymore either. If you don't go, I'm moving out."* She had tears in her eyes, and I know it was hard for her to say, but I felt that familiar guilt I've worked so hard to avoid, and I just wanted to get away from her. If not physically, then mentally. I took a quick look at the flyer she handed me and had to stop myself from crumpling it into a ball and throwing it back in her face. I don't usually get mad at Luci, but I was definitely teetering on the edge of anger. I felt deceived by her. Who was this traitor in Luci's body?

The bouncer from my bed slithered out of my room, grumbled a quick, "See ya later" and left. I had completely forgotten he was even there. My mind wandered to the naughty evening we shared together, and I wondered if there was any more of that smooth, purple weed left. It was too early to deal with the bomb Luci dropped on me. Without a word to Luci, I turned away with my flyer in hand and headed back to my bedroom. I sat on my bed and looked around my night table for any leftovers from last night's boy toy. Aha! One lovely, little roach containing just enough weed to erase my morning for a little while. I took the last hits off it and then laid back and waited for the tingles to come and take me away to a place where Luci couldn't find me.

As I slept the day away, I dreamed of Callie. It wasn't the nightmares that drive me into a drunken stupor but the kind of dreams that leave me feeling like she was in my room, stroking my hair as I slept. These are the kinds of dreams that I never want to wake up from:

"Wake up! It's Easter. Wake up, wake up, wake up!" I was jumping on and tickling Callie, insisting she arise so we could run downstairs to begin our favorite Easter tradition. The Egg Hunt.

"I can't believe Mom and Dad still hide eggs for us," Callie laughed as we raced down the stairs pushing and elbowing each other,

so we could be first. We poked around cupboards and tore cushions from the couch looking for the plastic eggs they'd hidden for us as they did every year since we were tiny. Our parents thought we were nuts; two high school girls fighting over animal shaped erasers and candy.

"Don't forget, we split the loot from them! You aren't gipping me out of my share of peanut butter cups this year," I yelled as I zig-zagged past her and threw an elbow to her ribs, so I could beat her to the back deck where I knew there'd be at least twenty plastic eggs containing the much-coveted loot.

"Hey, ow! I call bullshit!" Callie yelled. I just laughed and kept running.

In a Roman Catholic, Italian household, Easter wasn't just the gateway to Spring Break, it was a holiday nearly as exciting as Christmas. There were days spent cooking all the traditional Easter favorites: stuffed artichokes, lamb, Easter pie, deviled eggs, lamb cake (this is not a cake made from lamb rather a cake in the shape of a lamb), ricotta cookies, and of course no holiday meal was complete without gnocchi, meatballs, and Italian sausage. Our house would be near bursting with family and decorated in crosses made from palm fronds. The smells seeping from our house made the neighborhood drool.

After the Easter egg hunt, we'd all get dressed in our best spring outfits and head to church. It was exciting – the whole parish seemed to be humming with excitement. The organ seemed to be playing louder than usual, and the choir sounded less like middle-aged school teachers and a little more like angels. The smell of Easter Lilies was thick in the air, and it mixed with the smell of our mother's perfume in a way that made us nuzzle into her neck to drink in the smell during the service. She'd make a show of trying to get our heads off her shoulders, but she didn't try very hard. We knew she liked it.

This particular Easter was about a month after a very bad thing happened to Callie. It was the first time she had to be around our entire extended family, and I wasn't sure how she would handle it. I felt like she was starting to be more like her old self, but old, Italian ladies can really test your patience if you aren't in the proper mood. There's all the "You're too skinny. Do you have a boyfriend? How's school? Your Great Uncle Sal passed, God rest his soul. Are you losing weight? Did

I mention you're too skinny? Bring your old aunt another glass of wine," questions, comments, and requests. I love them all, but they can be a lot. To my delight, Callie was on her A-game and chatted up our aunts and Nonna with her usual charm. It was amazing how easily she could turn it on and seem completely normal and happy. I wore my emotions on my sleeve, so I mostly just looked worried all the time, which inevitably led to the "Why do you look so worried? Don't scrunch your forehead, you'll get wrinkles. Maybe she's constipated. You should eat more fiber." Questions and comments.

Once Easter was over and all the excitement had worn off, we endured the inevitable let down after the end of a holiday. We had a week off of school for Spring Break, but we weren't going on trips like so many others; our parents couldn't take the time off of work. We did a lot of binge-watching TV and eating junk food for a couple of days. Our mom became disgusted with us and decided we needed a project, so she had us sort photos and put them in albums. We did a lot more oohing and ahhing over how cute we were as babies than we did actually sorting, but it was great looking at old photos and talking about all the good times we had, or didn't have, on family trips. We made fun of each other's bad outfits and haircuts from the old days and laughed until our stomachs ached from it.

After we grew tired of looking at pictures, we chatted about Callie's upcoming graduation, and of course, prom. "Do you think you'll still go to prom?" I asked.

"I'm not sure. Part of me wants to show everyone that they can't keep me down, but I'm not sure I can handle an entire night of glad-handing and being fake nice to a bunch of assholes I hope I never see again. I don't even know who I'd go with at this point."

I wasn't the prom kind of girl, not really, but I wanted to see Callie "get back on her horse" and outshine all those jerks at our high school that crapped all over her. I was a junior, so I was technically invited to prom anyway.

"Well, what if I went with you? Do you think you might want to go then?" I asked.

She thought for a minute – I could see her wheels turning - and then declared, "You would make the very best date! Let's do it – 'The Mancini Sisters Take on Prom.' We'll have the best time."

Callie hugged me and twirled me around the room until I was dizzy and I needed to sit back down.

"What do you think you'll wear?" I implored.

She shrugged her shoulders and replied, "I'm feeling vintage-y."

"What the hell does that even mean?" I questioned.

"I want something that suits me perfectly and that nobody else will have. I'm pretty sure I was a celebrity in a past life - I want to look like an old time-y movie star," she explained.

I wasn't quite sure what she meant, so she flipped through some of the old pictures of our parents until she found some of them at a New Year's Eve party long before we were born. I couldn't even guess at the year, but my mother was wearing the most beautiful mint green dress. The silk hugged her in all the right places, and you could see the joy exploding from her as the photographer captured her in mid-laugh with her head thrown back and her arms around my dad's shoulders. She looked like a movie star, and I imagined that all the men at that party were stealing glances at her and wishing they were my dad. I could see, just from this picture, where Callie got her inner-sparkle.

"Well, we have the rest of Spring Break to find it. Where should we start?" I asked.

"Not around here. That's for sure. We should go thrifting and boutique shopping!" Nothing excited Callie more than a good shopping spree. "We could take a road trip, like the old days – just not with Mom and Dad. I know they won't let us go too far, but considering most of the kids we know are in Mexico for Spring Break, I think we can talk them into a couple day road trip in Michigan."

"That would be so fun!" I screeched in excitement.

"Sister trip!" Callie screamed in return. We proceeded to do a little happy, celebration dance.

If someone who didn't really know us would have walked in, they would have thought we were total lunatics, jumping on the couch and shouting "Road trip! Woot, woot!"

"Where should we go?" Callie asked once we were out of breath from dancing and jumping. I was so excited that I didn't care where we went, as long as we were together.

"I don't know," I replied. "Maybe we should just start driving and stop in places that look interesting."

"Yes! I love that. It's the ultimate Easter egg hunt...but for a dress!" she mused.

The next phase was the tricky part. How do we sell this to our parents and get the outcome we want? We strategized and schemed, and ultimately we just told them the truth. Callie was a senior and I was a junior; we were super responsible. We would keep toward the east side of Michigan and not go north of Oscoda; most of the other kids in school are in Mexico getting drunk and sunburned and we just want to buy a dress. Callie will leave for college soon, and we really wanted to spend some time together...Once we were done pleading our case to our parents, they went into the kitchen to have a discussion about it. We waited and waited, and they finally emerged with looks of resignation on their faces. I knew right then that we had won.

"You can go, but we want you back by Saturday and you have to check in with us at least twice a day," my dad explained.

"Yay!" we both yelled as we resumed jumping up and down. We thanked them and ran upstairs to pack before they could change their minds.

The next morning, we woke up bright and early, got ready, and grabbed our bags, so we could get on the road. As we left the house, we were giddy with excitement and our family dog, Daisy, looked at us like we were completely nuts. We pet her goodbye and headed down the driveway toward Elvis. No, not THE Elvis Presley but our beige Toyota Camry that Callie and I shared. We had a lot of arguments over our car, about splitting time and putting gas in it, but when it came to naming our beloved vehicle, we immediately agreed on Elvis – if our family loved anything as a group, it was The King of Rock and Roll. It wouldn't be odd at our house to find us all in the family room dancing and singing like spastic monkeys to "All Shook Up."

My dad popped the trunk and loaded our bags. After closing the trunk, he took a deep breath and said, "Don't forget to keep an eye on the gas level and check your oil and don't speed. Don't let anyone know you're traveling alone, and don't talk to strange men...or any men. No stopping at rest stops – if you need to use the bathroom, stop at a McDonald's. Keep the radio down, so you can concentrate while you're driving." He ticked off the rules to us as we smiled and nodded with solemn, responsible looks on our faces.

"We'll be good, Daddy!" Callie promised and then she kissed her index finger and rubbed it on his nose. It was the cutest thing.

"Call you later tonight," I added. I didn't have that same free spirit Callie had, so I felt weird trying to follow up Callie's adorable nose-finger-kiss-thing. I put my hand out for a high five, and my dad smiled and tried to swat my hand, but we totally missed. We both chuckled and he rubbed my head, making my hair stick out all over.

"Love you, girls!" my mom called to us.

"Love you, too!" we said in unison.

Finally we were off on our adventure, just the three of us, Callie, Elvis, and me. The sun was shining, the windows were down, and music was playing at a respectable volume as we backed out of the driveway.

After we pulled out of our neighborhood, Callie screamed "Yahoo!" out the window, turned up the radio, and punched the gas pedal. We raced onto the expressway like we were outrunning the cops. "I feel like I can breathe again. I'm so happy to get out of this asshole town!"

"I know. I'm so happy we're doing this...just don't crash us before we get to have some fun," I said with a nervous laugh. We sang loud to whatever music came on the radio, and Callie drove way too fast. It was exhilarating! For me being with Callie was a vacation from myself. Her personality was so big and she was so free, it gave me the courage to show a little of my loud, wild side because no matter how much I let loose, Callie always out-sparkled me.

We spent day one scouring boutiques and resale shops for the perfect prom dress. We stopped in nearly every town that we could easily find a re-sale shop. We tried on the most ridiculous outfits and laughed at each other as we put on stupid hats and walked our invisible catwalk.

"How do you like this one, Silvy?" Callie walked out of the dressing room in a floor-length, poofy-sleeved, butter yellow dress with brown and yellow vines of flowers in columns from neck to hem. She strutted and spun, and no matter how ugly that dress was, she made it look beautiful. We must have taken a hundred pictures of the two of us in polyester pantsuits, frilly dresses, and all sorts of undesirable clothing discarded by strangers. My favorite by far was the gold lamé jumper with a halter top. Everything about the jumpsuit was a shit show, from the fabric to the camel toe it gave me. I figured that maybe a retired hooker had dropped it at the shop as a donation. I'd never looked so ridiculous in my life.

When we were done shopping on our first day, we stopped off for matching manis and pedis, purple on our fingers and blue on our toes. While our feet soaked and our fingers were perfected, we read gossip magazines and talked about who was going to prom together.

"I can't even believe that Sarah's going to prom with Mark after all the times he cheated on her. I think she thinks she'll be voted prom queen if she goes with him. It's pathetic," Callie explained. Sarah was the first friend to turn on Callie after the bad thing that happened, I mean really turn on her. She was cruel to Callie's face and talked behind her back to anyone who would listen. I think she was trying to impress Callie's ex-boyfriend, Gabe, thinking she stood a chance at dating him since Callie was out of the picture, but he never even noticed her that I know of, so she crawled back to Mark.

After our polish dried, we walked around the town until we found the cutest old-fashioned ice cream shop. We popped in and had ice cream for dinner – chocolate peanut butter for me and strawberry for Callie.

"Should we get a motel room, Cal? I'm pretty beat," I asked as I tried to wipe the sticky ice cream from my chin and hands.

"Sure. Let's see what we can find." We hopped in Elvis and drove around until we ended up at a rundown motel that I was sure they usually rented by the hour. However, it was within our budget, so we called it home for one night. After we paid cash and got the key from the probable pedophile at the front desk, we headed to our room.

"The Royal Den. Huh. More like The Soiled Den. This place is so gross!" I whined.

"No complaining! We'll just get the blanket out of the car and lay it on the bed. Just don't actually touch anything; you never know where that creepy hotel manager whacks off!" Callie made a crude gesture that included her fist pumping back and forth below her waist as she rolled her eyes and made moaning noises.

"Ew! He's so creepy, you're probably right!" I made gagging noises, and we both laughed hysterically.

We called my parents as promised and assured them we were safe and sound. After the call, we decided the ice cream only served to make us hungrier, so we drove to a local diner where Callie worked to break all of my dad's rules as best she could. She charmed the manager with tales of our day spent shopping and told him about our nasty motel. I don't think he gave a rat's ass about our day, he just liked admiring the way her shirt hugged her curves and having the attention of a girl as beautiful as Callie. After our late second-dinner, we headed back to The Soiled Den. We climbed onto the blanket that we spread on the bed and did our best not to roll off of our protective barrier and on to what we were sure was a semen and bed bug filled quilt. We turned on the TV and watched old episodes of Bewitched until we fell asleep.

We managed to get a decent night's sleep without being infested with cooties, but we thought it would be pushing our luck to try the shower. After changing our clothes and freshening up, we headed out to finish our quest for the perfect prom dress. Early into our day, only our second store, we found the perfect dress in a tiny town near Lake Huron. I think my heart nearly stopped beating when Callie came out of the dressing room in the backless, barely pink, shift dress. It had beautiful iridescent, teardrop crystals sewn all over it, and when she spun, they sparkled and spread out like a flapper dress. I thought the sun must surely be jealous of how much she shone in that dress. It was stunning. To me nobody had ever been more beautiful than she was wearing the garment of her dreams. It was exactly what we'd been searching for, but it was also a little more expensive than what Callie had budgeted, so I gladly paid the difference because that dress was made for her. It was worth every cent of the babysitting money I had saved.

As we were checking out, I noticed a rack of necklaces near the register. They weren't vintage, but they were pretty. I picked one up that had a rose gold chain with a dark gray crystal heart, and I must have really looked like I wanted it because Callie nudged me as she walked by and told me not to over-think and to just buy it. I looked through a few more necklaces and found a matching necklace with a light pink heart, and I thought for a second about how great the necklace would look with her new dress. I grabbed them both when she wasn't looking and checked out. We walked out of the store, and Callie hugged me hard.

"What was that for?" I asked.

"Just 'cause I love you." She shrugged and winked. "Thanks for investing in my dress. I'll pay you back; I promise." We loaded our purchases into Elvis and then slowly made our way back down state, toward home. We stopped along the way for lunch and talked about the best way to wear her hair with her new prom dress. I could tell some of the wind had gone out of her now that the excitement of searching for the dress was finished. I began to realize the trip was a distraction, and a great one, but now that it was over, she had to go back to our normal life. We continued our trek home, and once we got close to our town, Callie grew increasingly quiet. She gave me a smile as we drove the last part of the trip, and I tried to encourage her to sing "Tainted Love" with me when it came on the radio, but she just smiled a hollow smile, and I could tell she was far away again.

Over the rest of the week, Luci and I were civil to each other and even had a few random laughs, but Luci spent most nights at her boyfriend's place, and I worked my usual bar shifts. It was quiet in the apartment without her; I missed knowing she was there if I needed her or just wanted some company. When I wasn't working, I locked myself in my room and smoked pot and watched movies from the eighties – they're my favorite. Beaches, Steel Magnolias, Mystic Pizza, St. Elmo's Fire, The Princess Bride, Sixteen Candles, Weird Science, Breakfast Club, National Lampoon's Vacation, Better Off Dead...I like almost anything from back then. For most of my week alone, I stayed off the booze – just trying out sobriety to see how it felt, but after that week's Friday night shift, I got completely hammered by myself on wine and vodka – not mixed together, that would be disgusting. I started with the last few shots of Tito's I had and then moved on to the bottle of rosé that I bought for Luci - it looked so lonely just sitting there in our refrigerator. That was the night I finally checked my email and clicked the registration link from Luci.

Chapter 3

Then - Luci

I can't imagine my life without Luci in it. She is smart, strong, funny, and my unwavering champion. I went to a small Catholic School called Holy Redeemer when I was growing up – the kind of school attached to a church with only one classroom per grade. Half the teachers were nuns and the other half was made up of ladies, young and old, and one man. The male teacher taught eighth-grade, and he was funny and exciting; it was like a gift to have him at the end of your nine-year sentence. A prize for making it through all the other teachers. Being at Holy Redeemer made me feel claustrophobic, and I felt like I never really fit in with the kids. Most of the kids were what I considered rich, while we were just comfortably middle-class. My mom thought being in a smaller environment would help bring me out of my shell and give me a chance to have more attention from my teachers. She thought I'd get lost and overlooked in the public schools. But I was so uncomfortable with those private school kids and teachers, I never felt like I could be myself. The best day of my pre-pubescent life was when Luci walked into our school in second grade. She was pretty and confident and just different from all the other girls; she had this fire in her eyes that I think only I could see. She reminded me of my sister in that way. I knew right away she was the kind of girl I wanted to have for a friend. For the first week or so after she arrived, I kept myself satisfied with small waves and shy smiles at her. Finally one day I was swinging by myself at recess (I was almost always by myself at recess), Luci approached me and asked if I wanted a push. I nodded my consent and then held on tight while she wound up to give me a giant push. From that very wiggly under-dog push and on, we were inseparable. At last I had found my person.

Luci and I were both outcasts, but we were outcasts together; me because I was shy and awkward and didn't particularly care for brushing my hair, and Luci because she looked different and came from a less affluent area. Luci has a white mother and an African-American father. The kids in our school didn't quite know what to do with diversity at that time; they weren't bad kids, and I'm sure that most didn't turn out to be giant bigots, but they were young and couldn't get past the fact that the new student in our class had darker packaging than the rest of us. Our town was pretty vanilla, but I thought she was beautiful – I envied her coffee with cream skin tone and in my seven-year-old way, wondered what I had to do to become African-American myself, so I could have that pretty skin. My friendship with Luci blossomed. and we spent most weekends having sleep overs and running around my backyard; we'd splash in the creek and climb trees until our hands would bleed. Sometimes her dad would take us roller skating, and other times we'd ride bikes to McDonald's and split large orders of French fries. In the evening, we'd put on makeup and do our hair to see what we might look like when we got older. Luci taught me how to stuff my bra with socks because I'd look more womanly with boobs – they were lumpy boobs, but I hoped someday I'd really fill out a shirt like that (only less lumpy). Luci would laugh at me when I'd try to tame her afro-styled hair and called me stupid when I would call my dry skin "ashy." She wouldn't get mad – she knew I loved her and just wanted to be a part of her world. Once we were all dolled up, we'd parade ourselves in front of Callie and my parents, and they'd laugh and roll their eyes, but they mostly told us how pretty we looked. I loved our sleepovers.

Through the years, we spent plenty of days in the principal's office for passing notes with swear words written in them or because Luci would tell off some boy who tried to lift my uniform skirt on the playground. In fifth grade, I truly understood that I could trust Luci to guard my heart. Our teacher was a pretty blonde lady, Mrs. Lund, and I thought maybe she'd be nicer and more understanding than some of the nuns we'd had as teachers because she was pretty and had a daughter at the school who was one grade older than us. She was thin and wore pencil skirts with beautiful high heels that made clacking noises when she walked. I thought she belonged in magazines; she seemed much too glamorous for that stuffy, old school. Unfortunately I learned quickly that just because the outside is pretty doesn't mean that what's inside is. Mrs. Lund turned out to be intimidating and had a clipped and condescending way of speaking that made my heart hammer in my chest anytime her attention was directed toward me. After being in her class for only a week, my ten-year-old mind was sure she was some sort of demon or vampire. Only a vampire could transform from something so beautiful into something so evil. I think she knew I was good prey – I was quiet and shy and didn't really stand up for myself. So when she would call on me in class, she would mimic me if I couldn't spit out my answers quick enough. I couldn't help the fear of saying something wrong and getting my head bitten off by her. She'd read my theme paragraphs out loud in class and point out all of my mistakes to the rest of the students – this isn't something she did to everyone else; she saved it just for me. Oh, how she belly-laughed and encouraged the class to do it as well, when I wrote, "I ate the <u>hole</u> thing" instead of "I ate the <u>whole</u> thing" in one of my paragraphs she read out loud to the class. Wasn't I so stupid? Not even Luci could console me that day at recess; I thought I would die of embarrassment. Mrs. Lund was making it her mission to show me just how "not smart" I was. I was a doormat, and she was a shit-encrusted pair of cowboy boots.

A couple months into fifth grade, while the <u>whole</u> class was gathered in the reading area, Mrs. Lund announced that she had a few things she'd like to discuss with us.

"Boys and girls, we'll be changing our music period from morning to right after recess. Also, our bagel day is being moved from Tuesdays to Wednesdays, and I will need to have your orders and money in my hands on Monday mornings." Ah, bagel day; aside from Luci, bagel day was the best thing at the school. If you remembered to put your order in, you were rewarded with a warm, freshly baked, chewy treat on the morning of delivery. Unfortunately for Callie and me, our parents hardly ever remembered to sign our order forms and leave us money. Mrs. Lund continued, "Next, I thought we should assign nicknames for some of you. We have two Julies and three Abigails, so do any of you have any nicknames at home that you'd like us to use here at school?" We spent some time assigning nicknames. And then, "Silvia…" I perked up a bit – she was smiling at me, and I thought I was finally getting some positive attention from her. I guess I didn't see the venom dripping from her fangs… "I've done some thinking and decided that there is one more nickname I'd like to give out. From now on, we'll call Silvia DD…for Dizzy Dago, a very fitting name, considering she is usually confused." I was like an abused dog – cowering when she was mean and then rolling on my back and accepting some belly rubs *when I thought she wanted to be nice to me, forgetting for a second that I'd get whacked again…and then, wham! Most of the kids around me began to laugh, but I didn't understand what was so funny. After a second, I recalled a joke my dad's friend had told him right in front of me about a dizzy blonde. (Why can't the dizzy blonde dial 9-1-1? Because she can't find the eleven!) It suddenly clicked. It was me – I was the dizzy blonde. I suddenly understood this name was meant to humiliate me. To my dismay, in front of everyone, I cried great big, fat tears of humiliation. I sucked in heaving breaths and snot ran from my nose – I didn't have a tissue, so I had to wipe my nose on the sleeves of my white oxford uniform shirt. I imagined my tears filling the room and drowning Mrs. Lund; we'd see if she'd laugh then. But just as I was wishing for Mrs. Lund to drown and for me to float away on my river of tears to someplace where people were nice to me, something happened. Luci, my tiny but mighty hero, stood tall and let that bitch of a teacher have an ear full of the most vile words I'd ever heard. Vile…and beautiful.*

"No, uh-uh. Excuse me, but I don't know who you think you are or what the hell you're doing, but no teacher's suppose to talk that way to a kid. My daddy says respect earns respect. Why are you always picking on her? You're hateful! I ought to wash out your ugly, stupid mouth with soap…"

Luci continued on for another minute or so, including several swears and a couple more bad names I'd never heard before until Mrs. Lund's face turned the richest shade of red I'd ever seen. It looked like her head might pop – I was sure it couldn't be healthy for a person to turn that color. Mrs. Lund loudly slammed a hand on her desk and angrily condemned Luci to the principal's office.

"Enough! That will be enough, Miss Johnson! You've crossed a line. Come with me. Children, while I'm walking Miss Johnson to Sister Sarah's office, I expect you to find a book and read silently. I don't want to hear a peep from this classroom." Mrs. Lund snapped at us. We all sat wide-eyed and weirdly excited. This was the most drama our class had ever seen. My tears had dried, and I sat in shocked wonder at my best friend's bravery. I'd hardly ever heard Luci talk that way. She was usually quiet and well-spoken. She always told me that she reserved that way of talking for when she got confronted by other kids in her neighborhood. If she talked too nicely, they gave her a hard time, said she was a white-woman-wannabe, and it was already hard enough because she was half white in a black neighborhood. When Mrs. Lund returned, she was angry and made us do twice the vocabulary worksheets than normal, but at least she wasn't laughing at me anymore.

Sister Sarah must have called Luci's parents because a little later I saw them pull up and park at the curb. I could see them through the window - her small mother with porcelain white skin and long brown hair to her waist and her handsome, hulking father with his ebony skin...and his tail between his legs. Even from a distance I could see the humiliation he felt at being called in to the school. I thought it was terrible that he felt shame at his daughter's actions instead of pride for her strength of character and heroism. Now that I'm older, I understand that the area in which Luci's family lived was rougher than mine and that some people from my area were afraid of people from over there. Luci's dad had taught her from a very young age to not make waves, to show respect to the teachers and students, and try to blend in as best she could. Most of all, she should never yell or act in a way that would seem scary to the other students. Her dad was worried that when Luci let Mrs. Lund have a piece of her mind, she proved to this white school that they really did have something to fear from them after all. He desperately wanted a good education for his daughter, and he was terrified it would be taken away. I didn't see Luci for three long school days and a whole weekend, but in kid-time, it seemed like a month. Regardless of the scene that was made on my nicknaming day, the name "DD" stuck, and I felt very dumb and very alone until Luci came back to school. I could tell she wasn't quite the same; a little of her fire went out, but I could still see the embers there, and I hoped I'd see the fire burn again someday.

I never told my parents about my woes with Mrs. Lund or the kids in class. I wasn't afraid to or anything, it just never occurred to me that anyone could help me. Besides, knowing my mom, she'd want to "discuss it with me." My mother's discussions were something I avoided whenever possible – they were well-intentioned, but they were long and they were lectures, not discussions. She would want to go down to the school and make a whole big deal out of my nickname, and all I wanted was to run as far from it as I could. If I would have told her, I might have gotten out of that school, but there was no guarantee she wouldn't have just shoved me into a different Catholic school. I wanted out – public school or bust. I complained often to my parents about wanting to change schools, but I was just a kid and hadn't honed my skills of persuasion, so my mother wouldn't budge on the subject. She was an unshakable force for the side of Catholic school, so it seemed impossible that I'd ever convince her to allow me to abandon Holy Redeemer for North Junior High School.

Chapter 4

Then – The Price of Public School

Weeks before I was to start seventh-grade, Callie and I camped out in our back yard and stayed up most of the night talking. We laid on our backs, staring up into the night sky.

"Look at all the stars tonight!" I exclaimed.

"Yeah, it's a perfect night," she agreed.

"I like the big sparkly one right there." I pointed up to show her the one.

"Yep, that's a good one. It won't be there long though. The bigger and more beautiful the star, the quicker it dies. The good ones die young," she explained, sounding somber.

"That makes me sad," I said.

"That's life I guess." Callie went quiet for a minute and then asked, "Are you okay, Silvy? I worry about you when I see you at school all alone when Luci isn't around. I never wanted to embarrass you, so I never brought it up, but I hear what all the kids call you. You know you can talk to me, right? You need to stand up for yourself."

"I know, Cal. It's just easier to let them talk. I wish I could start over somewhere new, but Mom won't change her mind about public school," I lamented.

"Well, we'll see about that. We have a new mission; I can't stand to see you have such a hard time at school." Her tone sounded like a promise, but I didn't want to get my hopes up too much.

"Sisters for life?" I raised my eyebrow at her and gave her my crooked smile.

"Sisters for life," she responded with her perfect smile.

Like an angel from God, Callie found the magic words that got our dad's attention and made our mom waver on her stance about public school: Sports and Drama Club. Extracurriculars were not offered at our small school, so Callie spun a story of how she was dying to play tennis and volleyball, how she dreamed of performing in school musicals. I happened to know that Callie could take these things or leave them – she was just trying to help me. I wasn't interested in sports, but I could certainly be persuaded to play a season of volleyball or join drama club if it meant I could escape Catholic school. Good old Dad suddenly had a fire lit under him at the thought of having an athlete, or maybe two, in our family. He was, after all, quite the sports fanatic. The tides had surely changed now that it was three to one in favor of public school. I don't know if it was our persuasive argument or if my mom was just tired of fighting this battle, but after much argument and some deliberation, we were given a pardon. After Labor Day, the Mancini girls would be starting public junior high school. I was elated at the thought of becoming a North Junior High School Panther, but the thought of leaving Luci behind left me with a small hollow spot in my chest. I was nervous to tell Luci the news, but for one night, I pushed my guilt about leaving her behind to the back of my mind. Callie and I celebrated our win that night with all of our favorites: Faygo Rock & Rye, popcorn, and peanut M&Ms.

"You did it, Cal! I can't believe it, but you did it," I cheered.

"I couldn't have done it without your puppy dog eyes. You were good in there! I was proud of you for speaking up." We clinked our glasses filled with Rock & Rye, and Callie said, "Cheers to our next adventure!"

The next day, I picked up the phone to call Luci and break the news that she'd have to get through the last two years of Holy Redeemer without me, but when she came to the phone, she was sniffling, like she'd been crying. I never even got the chance to share my news during that call. Luci had much more crushing information to share.

"Silvia, I'm moving." *She hiccupped and started to cry harder,* "I'm moving to Ohio!"

"What? That's impossible, plus Ohio's the worst..." *I sympathized. You see, if you were from Michigan (and especially if you were from Michigan and cheered for U of M), you didn't move to Ohio or even visit it unless it was to go to Cedar Point. That's just how it was – there was always a big rivalry between the states.*

"It's more than that, Silvia. My parents are getting divorced," she whimpered.
"Oh. Oh, I'm so sorry, Luci."

"My mom is making me move to Ohio with her because of some job. I leave in a week." Luci started to ugly cry, and I sat there silent on the other end, not knowing what to say. My heart sank, and I felt like my body weighed 500 pounds. My dream had come true, but I was losing my best friend. Sure there were a couple of other misfits that I became friends with through the years, but Luci was my person, and she was leaving.

Luci and I spent every possible moment together until the day I stood in her dad's driveway and watched her climb into her mom's very old blue Dodge Omni that was packed to the ceiling with their belongings. They had strung mattresses to the top of the Omni, and they made the car look comically small, like a clown car. We said a final tear-filled good-bye and promised to keep in touch. Then they drove off toward I-75 South and their new life.

I'd check the mailbox every day to see if Luci had written, and when I was rewarded with a letter, I'd run to my room to devour the lines. Her writing was tiny and smooshed together and she dotted all her i's with little bubbles and colored heart and flower borders along the margins of the pages. These special touches reminded me that she still cared; I was still her best friend.

> Dear Silvia,
>
> I started school today. Public school! There are actually other black kids at my new school! I sat with a few people at lunch, and they were pretty nice. My clothes are the worst, but my mom promised to take me to the mall. I hope she'll let me get something from Abercrombie – fingers crossed! Not much to report yet, but I'll hit you up later and fill you in more.
>
> Have you started at North yet? Tell Callie I said hi. I gotta go. My mom is yelling for me to eat dinner. TTYL!
>
> LYLAS,
> Luci
> xoxo

Dear Luci,

Oh my god! I never knew what school could be like. The hallways are alive with everyone yelling and girls doing their make up in locker mirrors. Boyfriends and girlfriends holding hands and kissing. I love that everyone wears what they want instead of uniforms. I have a locker - no mirror in it…yet, but I have a locker! I made a new friend in my first period math class, and she says she wants to be friends with me because I'm pretty. I'm not sure what that means, but Callie's sure she wants me for a friend, so she can keep a leash on me because I'm prettier than her. Her name is Jenny, and she says my ears stick out and that I should wear makeup, so I sneak eyeliner and mascara to school and put them on in the bathroom. Of course Callie says she'll tell on me for wearing makeup unless I do her chores – I don't think she really would, but I do them just in case. It's totally worth it.

I don't have much to wear either, and the most my mom will do is take us to Target and Kohl's, but I did get the coolest jeans and some cute sweaters. Did you get anything from Abercrombie?

I miss you so much! Write back soon!

KIT,
Silvia

P.S. Callie says hi back!

We wrote letters like this to each other about once a week and were allowed to make occasional phone calls, so we kept in touch the best we could. Once home e-mail became mainstream, it made it possible for us to "chat" almost every day. We were there for each other through boyfriends, break-ups, fights with friends, fashion choices, her grandpa's death, and arguments with family. When I wasn't emailing with Luci or hanging out with my sister or my new friends, I was reading. I read every book I could get my hands on – I even read some of my mom's racy romance novels, which got me grounded for two weeks when she found one of them sticking out from under my bed - and spent hours looking up words and information I read in books that I didn't understand or never heard before. I was determined to show the world that I wasn't dumb like Mrs. Lund made me feel in fifth-grade. I was determined to expand my vocabulary and general understanding of the world. It turns out I had a real knack for vocabulary and psychology. It took me a little while to embrace that I am actually a pretty smart cookie, but once I did, you couldn't stop me from talking like a third-year psych student. Any time I would spout off extra information or make an unsolicited observation, my sister would roll her eyes at me and refer to me as Dr. Silvy, which was a huge improvement from Mrs. Lund's "DD."

The best news came when I was halfway through my sophomore year. Luci called me out of the blue – we usually planned ahead for our phone calls to make sure we were both available, so you can imagine my surprise when my dad yelled for me to take a phone call on a random Monday night.

"Silvia! I have the most exciting news!" I could tell, even over the phone, that she was bouncing up and down.

"What is it? Do you have a boyfriend? Whaaaat?" I, too, was bouncing up and down with excitement. I couldn't imagine what the news was that couldn't wait until our planned call Wednesday night.

"I'm moving home to Michigan! My grandma needs help keeping up the house now that my grandpa is gone, so my mom volunteered me to go live with her." The information exploded from her mouth like a rocket bound for the moon.

This news was bigger than her just moving back to Michigan; her grandmother lived in my school district, so Luci would be going to school with me. Thank God because without her, I don't know if I would have made it through my last years of high school. It seems the universe knew what I'd need to survive what was coming.

Chapter 5

Now - Personal Hell

The real me knows that Luci deserves better than me for a best friend. So now I'm here, willing to give the retreat a try if it will help me keep Luci in my life. If I'm completely honest with myself, I am hopeful this retreat will help me. I didn't admit it to Luci, but I feel myself slipping away, too, and it's scary.

    I had to fill out a form when I drunkenly registered for this retreat. I have a hazy recollection of the form asking me to describe my "Loss Event." Loss Event, like I've just misplaced my wallet or something… Now that I'm here and they've handed me my registration packet that includes my form as it was submitted, I'm pretty positive the bottle of rosé and lemon drop shots (hold the lemons and sugar) I had before filling it out were a bad idea.

    Name: **Silvia Mancini** Age: **25** Sex: **Not lately, lol!!**

    Address: **1148 Northstar Lane, Richton Hills, MI**

    Phone No.: **(222) 555-2132**

    Emergency Contact: **Luci Johnson**

    Phone No.: **(222) 555-8484**

Relationship: **The only person who really loves me or gives a shit if I'm dead or alive.**

Please describe your loss event: **My sister fucking died.**

How has event affected family relationships: **My mother lives in la-la-land with her second husband and pretends she never had children. My father is a drunk. So I'd say my family fell apart when MY SISTER FUCKING DIED.**

How do you hope our Loss Counselors can help you: **They can get me another drink.**

Aside from thinking how hilarious I am, I realize how bitter I sound… Do I always sound this way? It's sort of embarrassing.

I'm looking around the room to see if our "Loss Counselors" have associated me with this mockery of a registration form. It won't be hard for them to figure out since I'm wearing an enormous "Hi, My Name Is Silvia" tag on my boob. I can add this to my ever-growing list of things I regret and feel stupid for doing. I pretty much always feel stupid, like my skin doesn't fit right, so it isn't a new feeling for me, just an unwanted one.

Now people around me start moving toward seats like cattle being herded into pasture, and I shake myself to clear my head and realize the Grand-Pooba-Loss-Counselor is speaking and directing us to take a seat. I move toward the back row and hope that nobody sits next to me. Ah, just my luck, there are exactly twenty of us and exactly twenty chairs. How very exact of the retreat-planner-people. A very chipper, boisterous girl sits right next to me. I give her a tight smile, but I quickly turn my body away from her, hoping she'll get the picture that I don't want to talk.

"Hi! I'm Jodie. This is so great. I can't believe I am finally here. I don't know about you, but I can't wait to get started! I didn't catch your name…"

"Silvia," I mumble and turn my shoulder toward her, so she can see my name tag.

"I love that name. It's so nice to meet you, Silvia. I have a feeling we will be very best friends by the time we leave here!"

"Not likely, Jodie – I already have a best friend, and you are a total freakshow for wanting to be here, and if you don't tone it down a notch, I'm going to have to bust into the bottle of Fireball I hid in my duffle bag just so I can deal with you."

Okay, I didn't say that to her, but I wanted to. I laugh to myself – sometimes I crack myself up. This internal laughter has forced a smile across my lips, and I realize poor Jodie thinks this smile is for her. Shit. I don't want to lead her on and encourage her. I turn my body away from her again and hope that she'll stop talking at me.

"Oh, here comes Dr. Wilson. She is the very best in her field. I want to hear every word she says…" Jodie trills. She touches my shoulder when she talks to me; every third or fourth word, she reaches out to me and makes contact. I feel myself clench every time her hand comes for me. Does this woman really not have any type of radar or understanding of body language? It takes some very deep breaths on my part to keep myself from jumping out of my seat and swatting her hand away.

"Welcome, friends. My name is Dr. Marie Wilson. I'm thankful to be here. I'm thankful you are all here. Most of all, I'm thankful for this opportunity to heal. In your registration packets, you will find your agenda for this retreat. Please notice that you have been assigned one of four groups. Please take a moment to find your groups."

Everyone stands and begins shuffling toward group number signs that are displayed to the left of the seats. It's kind of a cluster-fuck with people scrambling around to find a seat in their number row – it's just one more thing that annoys me today.

Have you ever had a sick feeling that sweeps through your body and leaves you with a sour stomach and the hairs on your neck standing at attention? I have that feeling. I have it for a very good reason. As I make my way to the "Group 3" sign, I realize Jodie is following me. The hits just keep on comin'.

"I knew it! I could feel it in my bones that you and I were destined to be friends. I feel so much better having a friend in my group!" Jodie is practically singing as she exclaims this.

Shit.

I double-check my agenda to make sure I really do belong in Group 3. I do.

Double-shit.

Before I can react to Jodie, Dr. Wilson is back at the podium explaining, in detail, about our next four days together....

"It looks like you all found your groups, or as I like to call them...families."

Triple-shit...I don't have much luck with family.

"Each family will have a chance to experience all planned activities during this retreat. I'll take just a few minutes to introduce you to our loss counselors. If each member of my staff could raise a hand when I call out your name and expertise, I'd appreciate it. I'll be happy to take any questions you may have after the introductions."

At this moment, Jodie's hand shoots into the air.

"Please hold questions until the end," Dr. Wilson admonishes.

Jodie's hand slithers back down, and a small frown flickers on her face.

"Gary? Ah, there you are. Gary practices Healing Touch. If you haven't tried it before, you are in for a treat."

Um, Gary has a porn stache. How am I supposed to take him seriously?

"...Sheila? Acupuncture is Sheila's specialty. I can see many of you are bristling at the word 'acupuncture,' but I think you will be pleasantly surprised to find that you liked it once you're finished."

I'm a little worried that someone who is going to stick me with needles is shaking like she needs a scotch on the rocks at 8:00 in the morning. I wonder what's wrong with her...

"...James? Ben? Nancy? These fabulous people are your psychotherapists and will be helping me with your one-on-one evaluations and making themselves generally available to you throughout this process..."

Ooooh, helloooo, Ben. I'd like my own naughty one-on-one evaluation with Ben please.

"...Now what sets this retreat apart from any other is narrative therapy. This process is allotted two days, and all families will work on this at the same time. Each person in your family will tell you the story of what brought them here. You will each repeat your story until you no longer cry when you tell it. It's okay if you only make it part way through your story the first few times you tell it. Some people may stop crying sooner than others. This is not a measure of how broken a person feels or of how strong they are. We all move at different paces. Once you are no longer crying when you narrate, you can listen to and support the remaining speakers in your family.

On our final day of the retreat, we will meditate as one large group. We hope to give you some inner-peace, so you are sent home with a renewed focus. We want you to continue your work toward accepting your grief as part of you that you need to listen to and nurture.

It is a long journey to fully reach inner-peace; you will need to move forward in your life in a way that allows you to satisfy your emotional needs without self-destruction. Please be kind to yourself and others along the way. Everyone here, including your Loss Counselors, has experienced life-changing loss and overwhelming grief. You are not alone. I'm happy to take questions at this time…"

Jodie's hand shoots back up, and when she is called on, it isn't even a question, it's a statement, "I am so happy to be here! I read your book, and it has opened my eyes and heart. I'm ready to heal, and I sure hope I get a chance to get to know you in the process."

Suck up.

"Well, thank you. I'm happy to have you here and look forward to getting to know you." Dr. Wilson is subtly brushing her off, and although I am currently anti-Jodie, I'm not appreciating Dr. Wilson's camp counselor speech and clear reproach toward a member of my pretend family. I mean this shit ain't free; she can at least fake it while we're here.

"If anyone has any actual questions, I'll be happy to answer them now, otherwise why doesn't everyone please take their bags to their family living quarters and take a few minutes to unpack? There are locker rooms designated for men and women where you can freshen up.

Let's meet back here, in the community room, in sixty minutes."

Holy Hell. This can't be happening. I guess in my drunken fog I failed to read the fine print…I am sharing a room with four other men and women. There is no escaping my pretend family.

Chapter 6

Then - Family

Being given a pretend family feels like a burden, like a burden I haven't had for years. After Callie died and I went off to college, I cut my parents out of my life. It wasn't a sudden cut off, it was gradual. I stopped calling, they stopped calling, and then I stopped going home for weekends and holidays. It only took a year, maybe two, to fully alienate them. The way they grieved over Callie never sat right with me. I was a kid, and they weren't there for me. Nobody rushed to my room to hold me when I'd wake up in a cold sweat after dreaming of finding Callie. My mom didn't make me comfort foods and tuck me in on the couch with a big, warm comforter and bring calming tea for me to drink. My dad tried to be the dutiful father, but it was too much for him. He started drinking every night, and as time passed, he was drunk more often than he was sober. Seeing my dad turn from hero to zero was devastating; it was almost like another death in the family. My mom tried to stick around for a while, but her response to Callie's absence was to pretend everything was normal and never talk about what happened. After she left my dad and me, she was off with her second husband traveling and living the good life. I felt offended by her lack of proper grieving over Callie. It was like she was playing the part of grieving mother: scene 1 – shock and hysterics; scene 2 – funeral arrangements; scene 3 – fall apart and cry exactly at the right moments; scene 4 – church grief group; scene 5 – cheat on husband, leave him, and forget about dead daughter AND living daughter...and cut,- that's a wrap.

My parents weren't always a mess. When Callie and I were younger, they worked a lot and didn't get to spend much extra time with us, but they tried to do things right when they were around. Our dad was the quintessential, overprotective father who would put the fear of God into any boy that looked at Callie or me (usually Callie). He was the most amazing shoulder to cry on, and when he would scoop us up into his strong arms, it felt like nothing bad could ever touch us. And our mom was so kind and beautiful. She was the type of person that would nurse a fallen bird back to health and feed stray cats on the back porch. She never squished a spider that wandered into our house; she'd trap it and release it back outside, so it could "find his family." Best of all, our parents were silly. They could make Callie and me giggle until we nearly peed our pants just by using silly voices and chasing us around the kitchen with wooden spoons, like they were trolls ready to cook us and eat us.

Our mom was so beautiful. When our parents had a date night, Callie and I would sit on the side of the bathtub for an hour just to watch her transform her already pretty face and hair into an award-winning masterpiece. We'd ooh and ahh when she put on a dress and high heels and then spun in circles, modeling the finished product for us. My dad would walk in and whistle at her as he twirled her around.

Then he'd say, "I sure am a lucky guy."

Our Nonna would come over to babysit, but our house acted like a sedative for her, and she'd be asleep on the couch by 8:00 P.M. every single time. After she fell asleep, Callie and I would pull out our mom's favorite red Betty Crocker cookbook and start stacking all the ingredients on the counter to make a chocolate cake. We'd mix and grease and bake and ice until we had a lopsided, half-eaten, chocolate mound to display. We'd use rolls of toilet paper like streamers to decorate the kitchen. When we were finished, we'd place the cake on the kitchen table, and by the time our parents would come home, we'd be hiding just out of sight. As soon as we'd hear the keys jingle in the lock and the door creak open, we'd pop out and scream, "SURPRISE!" We did this almost every time they went out, and to our parents' credit, they feigned surprise each and every time. They'd lavish all kinds of attention on us and sit and eat a piece of cake, no matter how terrible it might have tasted.

You also couldn't beat our summer vacations. My parents knew how to plan, and they always found the best places to visit. They'd take two weeks off of work, and we'd pile into my dad's big rectangle of a Cadillac and head off on a great adventure. We went all over the place. Sometimes it was up north

Michigan, near Traverse City. Other times we'd head to the East coast or to Montana to visit relatives. When they weren't working, my parents knew how to have a good time, and we looked forward to these trips every summer. Family time with our parents was limited, but it was fun, and I believe they did their best to give us the extra time they did have. I know we would have happily traded in the big house, Catholic school tuition, and some of the "stuff" for more time with our parents, but that wasn't how it was. So Callie and I had each other, for a while at least.

Chapter 7

Now - Roommates

We walk into our family quarters, and I am greeted by white: five white cots and bedding, five white wooden lockers, white bean bag chairs, and fuzzy white rugs. I kind of like it; it's like living in a cotton ball. I begin to unpack and find myself wishing I would have taken a little more care in choosing the items I brought with me. I brought my standard yoga pants and jeans, so those are fine, but I'm second guessing my t-shirt choices:

black t-shirt that reads, "Shut the Fuck Up"

pink t-shirt with an adorable kitten giving the middle finger

plain white t-shirt, complete with coffee stains

purple t-shirt that simply reads, "Psycho."

None of these shirts scream, "I am listening and here to heal!" Thankfully I'm wearing a plain black shirt that I'll be able to wear again in a couple of days. I can wear the coffee-stained white one, and then I will have to make do with the least offensive shirt for the other day – hmmm, kitty or psycho?

I finish putting my belongings away and head over to the locker room to wash the coffee stains from my white shirt that I plan to wear tomorrow. As I walk in, I see Jodie chatting up another poor soul who looks like she could use some rescuing, so I step in and ask if either of them has shampoo I can borrow to clean my shirt with (because no, I did not pack shampoo or conditioner or toothpaste or a hairbrush…). Jodie rushes to my rescue, and her captive runs free.

Now that we are all moved in together and have freshened up, we head back over to the Community Room. We've been tasked with getting to know one another, and memories of awkward childhood introductions flash before me. Of course Jodie has enthusiastically volunteered to introduce herself first. She gives all her particulars - her name, birthday, likes, dislikes, hopes, dreams, pizza toppings, yada, yada. I'm looking at the rest of my group to see if anyone else sees how annoying Jodie is, but everyone is smiling at her and sipping coffee like she is completely normal. Hmmm…The rest of us get up one at a time and introduce ourselves. Everyone seems to be nice enough, but I'm still not thrilled about getting so personal with them. Our group consists of Jodie, Diego, Tammy, Thomas, and me. Upon first inspection, I gather the following: Jodie is a plump, over-eager, suck-up, teacher's-pet type. Diego is a quiet and mysterious older guy with an accent. Tammy seems sweet with a touch of social anxiety (which I can completely relate to). Thomas seems like the kind of person I'd want for a best guy friend – cuddly, funny, and very smart, and then there is me, an angry, sarcastic loner with trust issues. We make quite an assorted family to say the least.

Chapter 8

Now - Retreat Activity No. 1; Evaluations

Our family's agenda puts us in line first for one-on-one evaluations. I'm sort of happy to get this out of the way. We follow the signs toward evaluation and find ourselves in a long hallway that leads to a really nice courtyard dotted with trees. On the left end of the hall is a partition, and I assume that's where we will be evaluated. To the right end of the hallway, there are chairs and iPads with headphones; this must be where we are supposed to wait our turn, so we head over and mill around like lost puppies. Our therapist eventually pops his head out from behind the divider and asks for his first victim. I give the biggest internal eyeroll possible at his weak attempt at humor and then volunteer to go first. Waiting in line to do things like this makes me anxious, so I'd rather just get it done. I am beckoned by our counselor to follow him behind the divider for our session while the rest of our group waits down the hall. There is a giant, fluffy beanbag behind the divider that I am directed to sit on, facing him. I'm startled when he sits in front of me and takes my hands in his, mine on top and his underneath, like we are going to play that hand-slapping game that I'm so terrible at. Where's the easy chair or couch to lie on? This set up is really unexpected. We weren't assigned to Ben as I'd hoped; we got James instead. He seems semi-normal, but I could live without sitting on a bean bag and holding hands with this guy, who, let's face it, needs some serious hand lotion and maybe a breath mint. I'm staring into his eyes, and I can tell he is present, here with me, ready to help. He begins speaking to me.

"Hello, Silvia. My name is James. If you don't mind, I'm going to ask you a series of questions, but please feel free to interrupt me if you need a break or if you need to steer the conversation in a new direction."

I nod and take a deep breath, hoping that I can let go of some of my sarcasm, so that I can take this seriously. I picture Callie's beautiful face and ask myself how she would handle herself in this situation. She'd probably flirt a lot and then turn the conversation around and find out all about him. I don't have that super power, so I exhale some bitterness and inhale again, hoping to fill my lungs with positivity and bravery.

"I've read your registration form; can you describe what you were feeling when you wrote your answers?"

I immediately feel my face flush. I knew that damned form would come back to haunt me.

"Well, to be honest, I was feeling drunk and stoned." This comes out more sarcastic than I intend.

James gives me a warm smile and clears his throat.

"That explains a lot. Is that something you do often, get drunk and stoned?" he asks.

"Yeah," I say simply.

"When do you find you drink or smoke pot most often?"

"Mostly when I feel alone, which is a lot. Sometimes after my bartending shift and other times when I can't get things off my mind and I just want to sleep," I answer.

"Is there anything, aside from alcohol or drugs, that could make you feel better when you are feeling down?"

"Well, my best friend makes me feel better sometimes."

"Can you tell me a little about your best friend?" James prods.

"Her name is Luci, and she just gets me. I've known her since second grade, and she is the best person I know."

"And what does Luci have to say about your moods lately?"

"She's sick of how I've been acting. She's dealt with it a long time, and I think she's tired. My bitterness bothers her; she's a 'glass half full' kind of girl, and I know my moods can be a real downer for her. She's the main reason I'm here, so I can pull myself together so she can love me again," I explain.

"You think she stopped loving you?" he asks.

I'm starting to feel a little exasperated. Every time I answer, I feel like he questions my answers, and I feel like I can't please him.

"I don't know. She doesn't love me like she used to, and I don't make it easy for her to like me. I think she stays with me and loves me out of obligation now because of our long history together."

"I see. So how do you feel when you are around Luci now?" he continues.

"Like I'm not a good enough friend to her. I say I will do things with her or for her, and then to make sure I can function socially, I drink or get high to loosen up and then I mess everything up. Like Luci has this new boyfriend, and I think my behavior when he is around embarrasses her. I just feel bad."

"Guilty?" James asks.

"Mmm, I guess. I don't know. I guess I feel guilty when I see that I cause her pain or frustration. I don't want to make her feel that way," I respond.

"Go on," he prods.

"I don't know. I think maybe I'm a little jealous. She spends a lot of time with this new guy, and I'm afraid she'll forget about me," I admit.

"And how is the dynamic between the three of you?" James inquires further.

"Not great I guess. They invite me out with them sometimes. If we all go out, I usually get drunk and do something stupid that pisses off the new boy and embarrasses her. I don't think he likes me; I haven't made much of a good impression when he's around," I explain.

"So aside from some jealousy, how do you feel now that your friend has someone else in her life?"

"A lot more alone now that I have to share her with him. I feel a little left out, or left behind, or something."

"Abandoned?" he asks.

What is this guy's deal with labels? Ergh! Inhale positivity, exhale negativity. Okay, I have to really think about this because I never considered this word before – abandoned. I roll it around in my head to see if it fits, and I think I hate this word; maybe this is my label.

"Maybe. Maybe a little I guess."

"Have you felt abandoned in the past?"

I feel a little sick. James is taking a path in my life I try not to travel – can't he see the police tape? Stay out. Danger! He did it so slyly that I hardly noticed, but now he's hit a nerve.

"Yeah," I croak.

"Who abandoned you?"

"Everyone," I snap.

James is calm and even-toned, "Who?" I hesitate and then I feel something wash over me. It feels like intense tingling that starts in my head and spreads through my body and limbs. My breathing becomes labored, my mouth feels sticky, and I don't feel well at all. Just as I start to suspect I'm having a heart attack, James senses what is happening; I think he can feel the pulse in my wrists, and he gently rocks our hands side to side and he's whispering something to me…"Stay with me," he repeats this several times in the softest voice I've ever heard. "Now breathe in deeply through your nose and slowly out through your mouth," he instructs. I think I'm breathing, it's hard to tell, but I must be because he says, "That's it, that's really good. Keep breathing and name something you can see."

I stammer something inane; I think I say, "Floor."

"What can you hear?"

"Static. I hear static." I remember there is a white noise machine running.

"Tell me what you can feel, Silvia," he pushes on.

"Your hands, I can feel your hands under mine." I'm feeling better, and I realize he has helped ground me, and my body doesn't feel like it's floating away anymore, and the tingles have mostly subsided. I feel a tear escape the corner of my eye, and before I know it, there are tears streaming down my face. It's like a saltwater volcano has erupted. I think I'm having a break-through moment – I've read about these or have seen them in TV shows. It seems so sudden, but I think I've wanted to do better for a long time but didn't know how to do it. The tears stop after another couple of minutes, and I silently vow to try to commit myself, the best I can, to this process. I'm tired of always guarding myself – building and holding up my emotional wall has been exhausting, and I'm ready to not hold it up anymore and let it crumble – at least a little. Maybe deep down inside this is why I signed up for the retreat in the first place?

James prods me gently and re-asks, "Who has abandoned you?"

"Everyone. My mom, my dad, and now maybe Luci if I'm not careful..." I sob.

"Who else left you?" he pushes.

"My sister," I squeak.

"How does that make you feel, Silvia?" His question is so gentle, I answer completely on instinct.

"Pissed. I'm angry. I'm sad and I'm lonely, and I'm just pissed off!" The volume of my voice raises an octave with each word until I practically yell the last part.

We talk a little more about Callie and my behavior over the last several years. But now I'm finished and am sitting outside in the courtyard by myself under a tree and enjoying some cool shade on my face and warm sun on my toes. This is the first time I've been by myself all day, and it feels delicious.

Chapter 9

Then - Dollhouse Massacre

I feel myself start to drift off to the smell of crab apple blossoms in the courtyard, the same type of trees Callie and I used to climb near the creek in the backyard of our childhood home. The smell takes me back to a more innocent time.

Calliope. It sounded to my five-year-old brain like a princess name. I hated that she got such a pretty name and I got a nerdy name. I'd never heard of a princess with a stupid name like Silvia. At least not until Callie told me a secret story about Princess Silvia of the Tree People whose super power was making trees and flowers grow at will and fought the evil people trying to cut down trees in the forest, so they could build stores. She was always doing things like that, making up stories to make me feel better. She instinctively knew what I needed to build my confidence. But she also knew just how to emotionally hit me where it hurt when she was mad at me. We didn't fight often, but when we did, it was ugly.

Callie was always emotional, and if she was in an especially volatile mood, she could get nasty. When we were nine and ten-years-old, I was obsessed with a dollhouse my dad made us with his own two hands. He had worked on it for months, and he had every detail of that house done to perfection. I recall so vividly the look of pride and satisfaction on my dad's face when he presented us with the dollhouse on Christmas morning. It was so perfect that I thought I heard angels singing as he unveiled it. I played with it nearly every day after we got it, but Callie wasn't very interested in it; she preferred writing in her diary and watching Bugs Bunny cartoons.

It was a warm spring day, and Callie was mad because she wanted to walk to Dairy Queen with her friends, but it was her turn to clean the bathroom, and she wasn't allowed to go until it was done. In true Callie fashion, she begged to clean the bathroom after she got back because her friends were leaving right away, but my mom held firm. Normally I wouldn't hesitate to step in and help out, so I could earn her praise, but I was planning on having Luci over to play and I was busy setting up my dollhouse – the mom doll was just about to go to the hospital to have a baby and Luci was bringing her old, pretend doctor kit, so she could help deliver the baby while the dad doll had an affair with the babysitter (my Nonna watched a lot of day time "stories," so I was well-versed in matters of marriage). Callie begged me to do it for her, but I refused. She got so angry that she shoved me, and I fell backward to the floor. I scraped my leg on the metal bed frame on my way down, and that is when my mom happened to be walking past my bedroom. I would have never tattled on Callie, but since my mom witnessed the shoving and my bloody leg needed some attention, there was no helping her out of trouble this time. Callie was sent to her room and grounded – no walk to Dairy Queen – nothing for two weeks, and she still had to clean the bathroom.

Luci came and went that day (you'll be happy to know the baby was a girl and perfectly healthy), and since Callie was a prisoner in our house, I sat on our backyard swing set by myself, doodling in the mud with a stick until it was time to go inside for dinner. When I went up to my room to change my muddy clothes, I was greeted by a dollhouse massacre. All the tiny dollhouse windows were smashed in, and each member of my little family of dolls had glittery maroon nail polish painted on its face, even the brand-new baby. It was, at the time, the single most tragic thing that had ever happened to me. I lost my mind and started screaming, then I stormed into Callie's room and launched myself at her. I scratched her and knocked down her Precious Moments figurines. I heard footsteps behind me and then I felt my dad's big hand grab my arm. I turned and hugged him as he lifted me up to hold me and I cried into his shoulder, leaving behind tears, mud, and boogers on his shirt. He demanded to know what was going on, so without speaking, I squirmed out of his arms and pulled him by the hand to my bedroom and pointed to my dollhouse. I saw a look of sadness pass over him – all that work destroyed, but it was quickly replaced by anger. I immediately regretted showing him. I knew Callie would be in deep trouble. In one fluid movement, he removed his belt and the threat he'd held over our heads for years but never followed through on was suddenly no longer a threat. He was in Callie's room in three large steps and then he put her over his knee and whacked her on her butt with his belt five times. He set her down, shut her door, and left without a word.

I stood in the hallway in shocked silence, wondering if it was safe to check on her. I decided to risk it, and I opened her door and found her laying on her bed with her face buried in her pillow. She didn't say anything, and I kept my mouth shut. I walked over and picked up her figurines that I'd knocked down and straightened some other things that were moved around during my counter-attack. Then I sat on the side of her bed and put my hand over her hand – she turned her hand over and gave me a squeeze, and right then I knew she was sorry about everything. I knew I'd never hear the words, "I'm sorry," so this squeeze would have to be enough for me.

I laid down next to her and whispered, "Sisters for life?"

Chapter 10

Now – Where's the Beef?

I must have dozed off under my tree because there are others in the courtyard when I open my eyes. Everyone seems to be inside themselves, probably reflecting on their sessions. I see my new, pretend brother Thomas sitting on a bench across from me, and I give him a wave. He walks over to me, cops a squat under my tree, and we sit in comfortable silence until he turns to me with so much seriousness in his eyes; for a minute I think he is going to confess his sins to me, or maybe propose.

He says, "I'm. Fucking. Starving." I burst out laughing. I wasn't expecting that from him, and I realize that I'm starving, too. "What do you say we walk over to the café and see what's for lunch?" Thomas asks.

I give a smile and nod my head yes. On the way over, we chat and get to know each other a little better. Thomas has a way about him that is so enticing, I find myself enthusiastically answering his questions and even asking some of my own in return. I have met only a few people in my life who can make me feel this comfortable, this quickly. And he's funny. I mean really funny, and there are real, honest laughs coming from me that I haven't heard in years.

"So how'd it go?" Thomas asks.

"Oh, it was all I dreamed it would be!" I mock. "How'd it go for you?"

"It was fine. I've been in therapy for years, so he was no match for me. I bet he got to you though. You have that 'first-timer' look to you. Don't sweat it, kid, it gets easier and it really does help," he explains.

"Yeah, it was rough, but I also kind of liked it. I feel so wishy-washy – one second I want nothing to do with this retreat and the next I'm registering for it. I felt really reluctant when we got here this morning, and now after one session, I'm suddenly looking forward to our next activity. I don't know what's wrong with me."

"Ah, don't overthink it. Just keep going with the flow and see where you end up," he advises.

"Aye, aye, Cap'n." I give him a wink and a salute.

When we arrive at the café, we get in line to grab some food and we notice, with horror, the lack of meat on the menu. There are lists of weird sounding dishes that highlight quinoa or tofu or chia seeds or all of the above. As I look around, I can't find a piece of cheese, a hamburger, or loaf of bread anywhere. I internally panic when I realize there isn't any meat anywhere; how will I survive without my daily cheeseburger? Thomas and I play it safe with grilled chicken salads, the only available poultry-containing dish in the joint. We take a seat at a table and start to dig in. We are a few bites in when the rest of our pretend family shows up and asks to join us. We nod our consent, and they all take a seat. Diego and Tammy played it safe with salads, too, but Jodie has chosen some concoction that features something unidentifiable to the rest of us. We all watch, enthralled, as she scoops a forkful into her mouth; we are staring to see if it is indeed edible. Jodie's face contorts as she tries to smile through her bite.

"Mmm. It's, um…chewy," she explains after she washes it down with Diet Coke.

We all laugh a little and decide it will probably be best to stick with salads for the remainder of our stay. We sit for a few minutes making idle chit chat. I'm feeling something I haven't truly felt in a long time. Comradery. It's a small, warm spot in my chest, and I can feel it starting to blossom and spread. These people are beginning to grow on me…a little.

Chapter 11

Now - Retreat Activity No. 2; Acupuncture

Tammy is pretty pale by nature, but she goes completely white and looks like she's going to throw up as we wait for the family before us to finish their acupuncture.

"You okay, Tammy?" I ask.

"I think so. I don't really like needles." I try to make her feel better by telling her that they aren't really "needle-needles," they are more like tiny pins, like what the *Hellraiser* guy has stuck all over his face and head. I don't think it helped her much because Thomas gives me a dirty look and begins talking over me. I guess I should work on my comforting skills.

"I think what Silvia is failing to say is that these are hardly considered needles at all. You can barely even feel them – it's not like a bee sting or a syringe or anything. I've had acupuncture, and it's more like you feel the tiniest prick and then pressure in the spot where the acupuncturist is working. If you breathe through it, it will be over before you know it," Thomas explains to Tammy as he gives her shoulders a squeeze of encouragement.

Tammy seems to take some solace in this, and she perks up just a tad. Before we know it, it's our turn for acupuncture, and I can now see that the acupuncturist (can't remember her name) has tables for each family member and she's changing the sheets on each one – at least she's sanitary. The tables are sectioned off with white privacy curtains all around them and a narrow walkway running length-wise along the tables, so she can access each person without having to leave the curtained area.

"Hello. You may remember my name is Sheila…"

Yes, that's right. Sheila! Shaky hands Sheila.

"Most people are nervous about acupuncture, but I can assure you that it is nearly painless. If you have a blockage in your chi, you may feel a deep, dull pain when I insert a needle into an area, but tell me immediately so I can relieve the pressure."

Sheila is reciting this information a bit robotically, but she has a nice smile, when she remembers to smile, and I can tell she loves what she does when she begins to explain what chi is. As she continues her explanation, the shaking leaves her voice and her hands begin to steady. I guess she was just nervous earlier, which makes her human, and that thought puts me a little more at ease.

"In Chinese medicine, chi is the spiritual energy that flows within the body. Acupuncture needles can treat specific problems, but today we will be working to improve your overall energy flow and treat any blockages we may find. I will insert the needles at all twelve main energy pathways. Each of these pathways is associated with major organs in the body. I know you may have many questions, but unless it is urgent, we will need to get started. Please select a table and undress from the waist up; ladies, this includes your bra. If you have on long pants, please pull them up above your knees, or you can remove them completely – whatever is most comfortable for you. Please lie face-down on your table."

With this she dismisses us to our tables. I am undressing, and I think that it's weird that the rest of my pretend family is getting semi-naked right next to me on the other side of the partitions. I can hear Tammy muttering in the section next to me. I think she's praying.

I whisper to her, "Remember to breathe. You got this." I'm on the far end, so I will be last to be impaled. I don't mind waiting my turn for this one since it doesn't require me to speak. I'm fine with needles, in fact I prefer being stabbed to speaking. I'd like to take a nap while I'm waiting, but I can't stop thinking about my evaluation with James. I really want to try to salvage my relationship with Luci. I remember when her mom moved her to Ohio – I missed her so much. I can't even imagine what losing her completely would feel like. I hear footsteps, and Sheila walks in quietly and lets me know she is ready to begin. The only thing that breaks the silence is the snap of rubber gloves as she puts on a new pair to work her magic on me.

I feel a prick and then a tap and twist – the first one must be in. Sheila works the needles into my body. It all goes pretty smoothly until she twists a couple in that hurt so badly, I want to jump out of my skin. I give her the signal that it's too painful, and she adjusts the culprits until I can tolerate them. When she is finished, she asks to see my tongue, which is totally strange.

"I know it's strange, but I can tell a lot about a person's health by their tongue," she answers like she read my mind. I ask her what she could tell about mine, but she tells me she will meet with me when I'm finished. She leaves me and returns later to remove the needles. "How are you feeling?"

"Umm. Okay, I think. I feel a little weird."

Sheila smiles at me and says, "For once weird is completely normal. You'll need to drink a lot of water today. Please take your time getting off the table and getting dressed; you may feel a little dizzy, that's normal, too. Give me a shout when you are dressed, and we can discuss your session." I thank her, put my clothes back on, and then call her in. "I hope you didn't experience too much pain?" she asks.

"No, not very much, just those few spots when I thought you were trying to kill me," I respond.

"I know, I'm sorry. The pains came from blockages in some pathways. I've written it down for you, but the pathways are 'Arm Yang Ming,' difficulty letting go; 'Leg yang Ming,' worry, nervousness, lack of acceptance, and lastly 'Leg Jue Yin,' anger, irritability, and depression."

"Yeah, I'll never remember that!" I laugh.

"The names don't exactly roll off the tongue, huh?" she laughs back. "Now when I looked at your tongue, I could see there is heat in your body, potentially the liver, and the coating on your tongue also indicates slow digestion. This session should have helped these issues, but if you continue with acupuncture once every week or two and drink detox tea, it should give you good results."

Sheila finishes explaining her findings, and when I walk out, my pretend family is waiting for me. I see that Tammy is still in one piece, and I'm glad to see that she made it out alive. I take a look at our schedule and see that we have been allotted a sixty-minute break to relax or meditate. I've got my heart set on finding my tree from earlier and catching a few more z's. I head, by myself, in the direction of my crab apple tree.

Chapter 12

Then - The Bad Thing That Happened

I never know what being sober and alone will bring me – I could be perfectly normal, or I could be assaulted by the past. This time? This time is bad for me. If I was home, I might smoke pot or have a drink – maybe both – to keep the ghosts at bay. But now I'm alone under my tree, and the ghosts are relentless.

When Callie was seventeen, she had a steady boyfriend, Gabe. Before Gabe she dated a lot but never had a serious boyfriend. Gabe was cute and pretty nice, but I didn't know him well. Callie was flirty with his friends, but she flirted with everyone – it was part of her charm, and it was innocent, and I thought most people understood that about her. Sometimes Gabe and his friends would come over to hang out at our house, and I'd hover, too shy to really participate but also secretly wanting to be noticed by the older boys. My braces were gone, and my acne had cleared, but my confidence hadn't developed. Gabe had one friend who was really good-looking, but he also made me super uncomfortable. His name was Scott, and I saw the way he looked at Callie, like he wanted to devour her.

Sometimes Callie would use our old childhood escape route to sneak out of the house in the middle of the night to meet Gabe, so they could make out. Sometimes Gabe would bring a friend, and I would go with her as her wing-man-girl and awkwardly chat with the friend while Callie and Gabe snuck off together. Some of the boys were really nice, and I even kissed one guy. I must have been a pretty bad kisser though; he never came back for more. The worst nights were when Gabe brought Scott. I would plead with Callie not to go off with Gabe on these nights because Scott gave me the creeps. She thought I was silly until one night, Scott tried to have his way with me.

 He was pawing at me, and I remember he said, "You're not Callie, but you'll do." Then he had his tongue in my mouth and his hand halfway down my pants. I managed to wiggle away a little and then I hauled off and decked him in the nose. He backed off and yelled, "You bitch!" There was a tiny trickle of blood seeping from his nose, and I felt completely satisfied and justified with what I'd done. Callie and Gabe came back from their make out session just in time to catch the action. Scott complained about me and said I was crazy, but I'd take crazy over molested any day. Gabe never brought Scott to his and Callie's rendezvous again.

 A couple months after Callie's eighteenth birthday, she and Gabe planned to meet for some alone time – I was not invited. It was only the end of March, but it was unseasonably warm and very muddy by the creek. Callie came into my room that night around 1:30 A.M. to tell me she was leaving. She had candles and a big blanket in her arms. She looked beautiful in a pink, plaid skirt, lace top, and her favorite Vans – she topped it all with a thick wool sweater. She said she was planning to lose her "V card." I had a weird feeling in the pit of my stomach, but I figured I was just nervous for her to do it with Gabe; your first time is a big deal, and I wanted it to be perfect for her. I asked her why she was leaving so early, and she said she wanted to set up everything, so that Gabe would be surprised. Callie was a such a romantic. I wanted to go with her and stay until Gabe got there, but she wouldn't let me.

 "Don't be silly, it'll ruin the mood. It's not very romantic if your sister sets up your sex scene," she said. I couldn't really argue with that. Callie left, and I fell asleep for a little while. I was dozing in fits, and at one point, I woke up to tapping on my window. I was disoriented and I thought there was a ghost outside my window. It took me a minute to figure out it was Callie. I was confused, why wouldn't she just come inside? I glanced at my phone to check the time and saw three missed calls from her. Weird. I threw on a sweatshirt and some shoes and climbed onto the roof. I started to ask her if she was insane, but thankfully before anything came out of my mouth, I realized Callie was not okay. She was pale, wet, and shaking. I hugged her to my warm body and rubbed my hand up and down her back. I think she was in shock or something because she had a vacant stare and she wasn't talking. I took her face in my hands and looked at her eyes until she focused on me. I grabbed her hands and was able to coax her into talking to me. She leaned in and rested her head on my chest, and I ran my fingers through her hair, trying to gently work out the knots as she told me what happened.

"When I got to our meeting spot, I spread out the blanket and started to light the candles I brought. I heard something move behind me and then arms wrapped around me. I giggled and started to say, 'You're early,' but I was cut short. I turned my head and gasped in surprise to see it was Scott, not Gabe. He must have seen the shock on my face; he tightened his grip on me and I could barely move." Callie stopped here and breathed for minute, and I realized she was still shivering. I coaxed her inside through my bedroom window and wrapped her in my Snoopy blanket. Once she warmed up a little and I soothed her some more, she continued her story. "Silvy, he pressed against me and I could feel on my hip how excited he was. It was gross and it scared me. I tried to make my face normal and play it off like it was no big deal. I said, 'Hey, you scared me. What's up? I didn't know you'd be here. I'm just waiting for Gabe. He'll be here soon.' I fake laughed and tried to pry his arms from me, but he was too strong." She sobbed and coughed a little. I could tell she didn't want to finish, and part of me didn't want her to. It was obvious to me how the story would end, at least the main theme, and it sickened me. "He was so quiet – it was creepy. He just stared at me for a while, and when he finally said something, he said the most terrible things. He told me that he sees the way I look at him and he notices how I flirt with him. He said he wanted to finally give me what he knew I really wanted." Jesus.

"I told him I was sorry if I gave him the wrong idea and told him that he was only a friend to me and that I love Gabe. But he wasn't hearing anything I had to say. It was like he was possessed." Callie was near hysterics again, and I knew she must be re-playing the horror in her head. I felt bad that she had to re-live it by telling me, but I had to know what happened, so I could try to help her, so I urged her forward. "He pushed me to the ground and started to tear at my shirt and lift my skirt. I hit him and scratched him, but he wouldn't stop. He just wouldn't stop. He just had this weird smile plastered to his face and he wouldn't stop. I screamed. I yelled, 'No.' I tried to roll away from him, and he slammed me back down. I scratched at his arms – I tried to reach his face – I wanted to shove my finger in his eye, but he was ready for that and kept himself just out of my reach. I kicked my legs, but I couldn't get him. Nothing was working. I was just flailing. I could tell he knew exactly how to do this – he'd thought it through - and there wasn't anything that would get *in his way.*" *My God, how many times has he done this? I wanted to kill him. The rage inside of me was building, and there was nowhere for it to go. I had to push it back down, so I could help Callie, but fuck, I wanted him to suffer.* "I was crying and begging him to stop, and that's when he finally went for it. He pinned my hands above my head and mauled at my boobs. He hiked my skirt up and ripped my underwear right off me. It hurt, and I thought to myself, 'I love those panties,' which is weird, right? Then he reached inside me with his fingers...He unzipped his pants and took what he came for..."

I sat there holding her. Both of us crying and me rocking her in my arms. What he'd come for was her dignity, her innocence. He wanted to make her feel small.

Callie finished her story, "When he finished with me, I was just lying there with all my parts hanging out. I didn't know what to do. I wanted to get up, but he was still there. I thought if I lay very still, maybe he'd just leave. Maybe I'd wake up from this and realize it was a nightmare. Then I heard him make a noise like he was disgusted with me. I continued to pray that he would just leave, and he started to do just that. But before he left, he spit on me and called me a slut. He kicked me hard in the ribs until I rolled away from him and into the creek."

I was picturing what she went through and I was horrified. She must have been so scared. He didn't just take her "V card," he took it, burned it, and then pissed on the ashes. To add insult to injury, she said Gabe never even showed.

When Callie was finished telling me what happened, she looked at me and whispered, "I lost my shoe." I was crying and nodding and telling her it would be okay, but I had a feeling it wouldn't be.

It was close to 4:00 A.M., and Callie was emotionally and physically drained. I asked her if she wanted to go to the hospital, but she was sure she didn't want to go. Just asking her made her go back into full panic mode. I took her in the bathroom and drew a warm bath for her. I sat on the side of the tub and gently washed her back and arms as she cried until she was empty. I inwardly thanked God that my dad was still at work and that my mom took pills that made her sleep like the dead. After washing her hair, I got Callie out of the bath and brought her to her room for some jammies. She asked if she could sleep with me like we used to when we were little. Of course she could. After I had her safely tucked in my bed, I snuck out and headed down to the toilet bowl to retrieve her missing shoe from the grate like she'd done for me when we were little kids. The toilet bowl is where the creek meets our city's drainage system. There is a big, metal grate that stops large debris from going underground with the water. The creek has a pretty good current in some parts but especially at the toilet bowl. The current there makes a whirlpool, so it looks like a flushing toilet. I was wishing I would find her innocence in that water, too, so I could give it back to her with her shoe.

When I went to school the next day, I was determined to corner Gabe and ask him where the hell he was the night before. If he would have met Callie like he was supposed to, Callie would be okay. Her V card would have been safely tucked in <u>his</u> wallet. I stopped by his locker between every class, but he never showed up. After school I detoured to his house before going home. Gabe opened the door for me wordlessly. He looked different, sad. Before I lost my nerve, I gave him a piece of my mind. I fired off questions without giving him time to answer.

"Where the hell were you last night? What the fuck is wrong with you? Why do you hang out with that sick fucker? How could you do that to Callie?" That set him off. His sadness turned to anger, and he spewed hateful words at me.

"How could <u>I</u> do that to <u>Callie</u>? Are you fucking kidding me? I was there, Silvia. I was late, but I was there. I'm not sure what the fuck has been going on behind my back, but I saw her with Scott. I was only a few minutes late, and when I walked up, I saw her and Scott going at it. I was so angry, I just left. If I hadn't, I would have lost my mind on them."

No, no. He had it all wrong! It was like a bad soap opera or made-for-TV movie. I tried to explain to him that he was wrong, that Callie loved him and that Scott hurt her.

The last thing out of my mouth was, "If you would have stayed, maybe you could have saved her." Then he slammed the door in my face. I knocked on the door again, but he wouldn't answer. I wasn't sure if I'd ever be able to get through to Gabe.

Callie was able to hide what happened to her from our parents with a little extra make-up and great acting – junior high drama club came in handy. She played sick for a few days and didn't go to school. I was at school though, and by the second day back after the night it happened, the rumors had spread like wildfire. I heard the whole story from Luci during our fourth period newspaper class. Scott bragged that Callie had always wanted him and that a couple nights ago she couldn't control herself anymore, so she begged him to meet her in the middle of the night for her birthday. So he did, and she fucked him like the slut she is. His only regret was that Gabe was hurt in the process. He said as *his best friend, he did Gabe a favor by showing him exactly what kind of person Callie really is. Did Gabe ever even ask himself why she would schedule a rendezvous with a secret lover on the same night, time, and place as she had agreed to meet Gabe? It was ridiculous, but the kids at school were eating it up, and apparently Gabe did, too. They were so eager to throw Callie from atop her pedestal that they were willing to believe whatever Scott said. They posted, texted, and whispered about her: Whore. Bitch. Slut.*

Gabe didn't officially break up with Callie, but he stopped calling her. When she finally went back to school, he ignored her. She could hear the kids whispering about her. Slut. She saw them laughing and pointing at her. Whore. Even the girls she counted as friends joined in the slut-shaming, or at best, they wouldn't make eye contact with her. Sarah was the worst. She heckled Callie in front of the whole lunchroom and spray painted "Slut" on Callie's locker. Sarah followed Gabe and Scott around like a groupie. It was sick. All the kids had a mob mentality, and they were attacking her with ugly words instead of pitchforks. It's disgusting, really, the way people love to see others stumble and fall, fail. I'm not wired that way; I'd rather help than hurt, so it was hard to understand how everyone could turn on her so quickly. I tried to meet Callie between classes and walk with her when I could, but I was a junior and she was a senior, so we didn't have the same schedule or lunch period. I'm not sure how she did it, but Callie kept her chin up during school and never shed a tear. I thought she was so strong, but she must have been laying plans in her head that even I didn't know about.

Chapter 13

Now - Retreat Activity No. 3; Healing Touch

Rest time is over, and I head to the small room designated for Healing Touch. The rest of my pretend family is already there waiting for me in the hall outside of the room. Porn stache guy comes out and gives us a huge smile, and I see he is actually quite attractive once you get past the stupid mustache. He asks us to sit in the chairs that have been set up in the hall.

"Welcome, I'm Gary. I'm sure that many, or maybe all of you, haven't heard of Healing Touch before. I like to describe it as similar to acupuncture in that we are working to clear disturbances in the body's energy system. Except, unlike acupuncture, we are working from the outside on the energy field that surrounds your body. This means no needles! Once we clear the disturbances, the energy channels are able to bring body, mind, and spirit together for healing. I will be bringing you in individually, and I ask that you lie flat on your back; there is no need to remove any clothing. I will use my hands and my intent to unruffle your energy channels. I may also lightly touch you at times. You may see me shake my hands; this is to expel any negative or disturbed energy that may have attached itself to me. I urge you to close your eyes and relax during your session, concentrate on your breathing, and meditate. When we are finished, you should feel refreshed and lighter."

I'm officially intrigued by Gary's introduction. I'm wondering if this shit actually works? I take my turn after Jodie. When she walks out of the room, she does seem lighter…hmmm.

I walk into the dimly lit room and lay down as Gary instructed earlier. I can smell the disinfectant he used to wipe the table. I'm still feeling pretty relaxed from the acupuncture and rest, meditating while Gary unruffles me should be no problem. He approaches me with warm, positive words and he begins to run his hands along an invisible path on my body. At first I'm so curious to see what he is doing that I don't notice anything, but then I feel it. I'm not even sure what "it" is, but it makes me completely alert and relaxed at the same time. I look closer and I notice he isn't touching me, but it feels like he is. I can actually feel him petting my energy with long strokes, like I'm a dog. There is a light buzzing feeling and pressure that comes with it. It isn't uncomfortable, but it's weird and it feels really personal. I feel a little giddy inside, like my body is humming in a good way. I try to relax while Gary finishes working on me.

Chapter 14

Now - Cocktails and Dimples...I Mean Dinner

It has been a long day, and it feels like I've already been here for a week. I'm looking forward to a hot shower and some food. I hope dinner tonight involves some meat.

When we get back to our room, there is an envelope waiting for us. Thomas opens the envelope and does a little happy dance before announcing that we have been invited to cocktails and dinner by the pool. Ooh, he had me at cocktails!

I had to settle for a lukewarm shower, but it felt good all the same. Now what the hell am I going to wear? Thomas and Diego are wearing cargo shorts and short-sleeve button down shirts. Jodie and Tammy are both wearing casual maxi dresses, and I'm standing in my bra and jeans wondering if my purple "psycho" shirt is proper cocktail attire. Tammy sees the worry on my face, and she hands me a black, lacy, short sleeve cardigan. It's not my style, but if I wear it with just a couple buttons done in the middle, it'll hide the word "Psycho," and the purple that shows through will give me a nice pop of color. Paired with my slightly dirty jeans, I look perfect-ish. I thank Tammy, and we head off to the party.

When we approach the pool area, I see there are plenty of other people who are in jeans, so I feel much better already. I begin scanning the area for the bar and...oh, good. I see it. I move to the head of our pretend family and make a beeline for the bar. To my dismay, there is no vodka or any other hard alcohol, only champagne cocktails. Better than nothing though. I down a first one standing at the bar and grab one in each hand before I walk away. I'm not sure if it was the acupuncture and Healing Touch, but something has made me a total light weight tonight; I can already feel the champagne spreading its numbing warmth through my body; it feels yummy. Diego snaps me out of my thoughts by asking if I want to go with the family to find a table. I follow my brothers and sisters in grief to a table near the buffet and grill. We review the menu cards that are sitting on the plates and find that we are having grilled swordfish for dinner. It's not a piece of cow, but it does sound delicious. I manage to finish a total of four champagne cocktails by the time dinner is served, and I'm feeling like I really need something in my stomach to help me sober up a bit. I don't want to alienate my pretend family on night one by drinking too much and making an ass of myself. I hope I'm not too late.

Dinner is delicious, and I try to focus on listening to Diego tell us about where he comes from in Mexico and what brought him to America, but the conversation has turned political, and I just don't have it in me to participate in such a serious conversation, so my thoughts begin to wander. I start to think about Luci. I wonder if she's packing all my belongings because she thinks I won't change, or if she's got new boy over and he's begging her to kick me out because I'm no good for her. God, what is his name? I'm so rotten, I never even committed his name to memory, or if I did, I shoved it so far back in my memory, it's afraid to come out. Right now I'm making a promise to get to know Luci's boyfriend better, or at least learn his name when I get home. If she really likes him, or loves him, I don't want to be the cause of any problems between them.

More champagne cocktails are served, and Dr. Wilson stands to make a toast.

"Here's to all of you and the progress I hope you've made today. May your journey here lead you to emotional freedom. Cheers!"

"Cheers!" everyone says in unison. This toast seems to be some sort of dismissal; several people head out and go back to their rooms. There are still some people milling around, so I start to head toward them because Thomas and yummy Dr. Ben are over there. On my way over, I notice the bartender is closing up shop, so I stop and talk her into giving me a couple opened but unfinished bottles of champagne that were going to be dumped out. I bring my prizes over to the group and pass one bottle around and hang on to the second. I join in a conversation about how tiring the day has been. I even interjected some opinions about the Healing Touch and how I thought that shit would never work but that somehow it did. I must have offended a couple people because they gave me judgey side eyes and left. Oops, maybe I've had a few too many cocktails…We hang out until the only people left are Thomas, Dr. Yummy and me. The three of us make a good dent in the second bottle of champagne, and Thomas announces he's "off like a dirty shirt."

I give him a hug and tell him I won't be far behind him and he whispers, "You're welcome" in my ear. He pulls out of the hug, winks at me, and says to Dr. Yummy, "Get my girl back to our room safely, won't you?" That Thomas makes one hell of a wing man.

I'm not sure what to say or how to proceed. I'm so bad at small talk when I'm not safely behind the bar serving cocktails. My face starts to heat up, and I need to say something now before I go completely red in the face and run off like Forrest Gump. I quickly knock back the rest of the champagne in my glass and go into my flirty bartender mode.

"So aren't you a little young to be a doctor? I mean you can't be more than twenty-eight," I ask with my best flirty voice.

He gives me a smile, showing off his perfect dimples, and says, "I'm not so young. I'll be thirty-one soon and I'm not a doctor…yet."

The overhead patio lights turn off all at once, like they are on a timer, and I start to walk toward the pool and sit on the edge in the near dark. I take off my shoes and dip my toes in the water. It's warm and looks so inviting; the way it reflects the ambient flood lights that are situated around the patio and the fairy lights in the trees. I can't control myself and I plunge my legs into the warm water, jeans and all. Ben laughs at me and walks over to join me on the side of the pool. He doesn't stick his legs in, but he folds his legs under himself and gets comfortable.

"So how was your first day?" he asks.

"Surprising. I had my first ever therapy session. I was stuck by needles and some guy pet my energy field like I'm a dog." I wink at him and giggle. God, what is wrong with me? I'm laying it on a bit thick, but I can't seem to stop. "But I actually liked it all more than I thought I would. You grief counselors are pretty smooth."

"Ha! You give us too much credit. I love my job though, helping people. Almost every day, I get the privilege of hearing pieces of people's history and helping them to deal with how it affects them. It's really gratifying." Man, he has the sexiest dimple in his left cheek. He's making it hard to concentrate…"So tell me about Silvia – are you from around here?" he digs.

"I am; I live in the village apartments just off-campus with my best friend. She found a local job after college, so we never moved away. Nothing too exciting to tell. I live with my best friend, I bartend, and I make bad decisions." I laugh and give a little unwanted snort.

This makes him smile, and I wonder if it is a smile that says, "She's so cute and endearing," or if he's just laughing at what a mess I am.

"Bartender, huh? What bar?" he asks.

"I tend bar at 'Charlie's' over on 12th Street. Do you know it?" I hate talking about my job because I'm twenty-five and still a bartender. I never finished college, and the conversation always turns in this direction. I'm not ashamed, but it's a little embarrassing to admit I quit just short of graduating.

"Yes! I haven't gone there in years. Do they still let you throw peanut shells all over the floor?"

"No, not anymore. Too many peanut allergies; now it's popcorn." He's smiling at me, and now I've got that warm spot in my chest again and my insides feel all liquid-y.

"Aw, that's too bad. I loved the smell of peanuts in there. So no big career plans then?" There. He did it. He took the dreaded turn.

I inhale deeply and in one breath say, "Nope. I was majoring in Psychology and minoring in Sociology but never managed to finish my bachelor's degree. I wanted to help people, but now I just get them drunk. Maybe one day I'll go back and finish, but I'm not ready right now."

"Shit happens. I get it," he says. Does he though, get it, I mean? I'm not even sure I get it. Once I got deep into my major classes, I started obsessing about Callie and what she must have been feeling for years. I questioned everything about her; about me, and how I handled things when we were kids. I was starting to be able to see what I couldn't understand when I was younger because I didn't know these things existed then: depression, mania, bi-polar. I couldn't take all the self-reflection and the thinking about Callie that my classes were leading me to do, so I quit.

I'm too much inside my own head, and before I can contain myself, I hop off the ledge and into the pool with all my clothes on. I feel a little guilty about Tammy's sweater the bottom of it is soaked, so I take it off and throw it on the patio next to my shoes, hoping the color doesn't fade. I smile up at Ben and then sink under the water, letting my long hair float around me. I'm reminded of the times Callie and I spent swimming together, pretending to be mermaids. They are sweet memories that I don't have to be afraid of; they don't chase me, they linger around me like an aura and hug me until I can't stay under any longer and I need to come up for air. When I come up, Ben is staring at me and he looks a little concerned.

"You okay? I thought I was going to have to jump in and save you."

"Come on in, the water's fine." I smile and give him my dreamiest bedroom eyes. He laughs, and there's that dimple again. Mmmm.

"As much as I'd love to, I think we better get back to our rooms. Long day tomorrow. Come on. Let's get you to your room," he says while he stands and reaches down to help me up out of the pool. Sadly I misread this situation, and when he pulls me up, I go in for the kill. I close in on him, and as my lips barely start to brush against his, he gently pushes me back and tells me that physical intimacy is forbidden between therapists and guests. I'm so embarrassed, I could actually die. If God is going to smite me, now would be a really great time for him to do it.

Yummy-Ben walks me back to my room in silence, and I realize I'm still quite drunk and very, very soggy. Every step I take causes my wet jeans to make strange fart-y-suction noises, and I hope he doesn't think I have uncontrollable gas.

When we get to my door, he says, "That was fun and…interesting. I hope we get to talk more before the retreat is over." I nod my head and give him an awkward smile and single-handedly open the door behind my back and slink into my room without turning my back to him.

Once I'm in my room, I realize I left my shoes and Tammy's sweater by the pool. But my cot calls to me and my forgotten items will have to wait until tomorrow.

DAY 2

Chapter 15

Now - Hot Mess

I'm out of bed…or cot rather. It was actually pretty comfortable, and to my surprise, none of my pretend family members snored like dragons or talked in their sleep. If they did, I slept right through it. I get up, head to the ladies' room, and peel my chlorine-soaked clothes off of me. I find my still-soggy white t-shirt that I washed in the sink yesterday and get ready for the day. I feel a little sick to my stomach, not sweet little butterflies but more like the man-eating kind that are attacking me from the inside. It's a mixture of last night's champagne (way too sweet), embarrassment, and nerves.

I'm sitting on my cot waiting for the others to get ready, and I can feel Thomas's stare from across the room.

I ignore him until he saunters over and says, "Soooo?" I look at him from the corner of my eye until I finally just tell him what happened last night, although I'm still quietly hoping it was just an awful dream. I can see by the way Thomas is screwing up his face that he wants to laugh at me, but he has manners enough not to. He simply says, "Oh, girl, you really are a hot mess, aren't you? What are we going to do with you?" I shrug my shoulders and then we gather the troops to head for breakfast.

As we walk out of our room, I trip over something sitting right outside our door. My shoes and Tammy's sweater. Ugh, last night was not a dream. Dammit. Ben must have noticed my shoes and sweater by the pool on his way back to the staff rooms and deposited them here. If it wasn't for the fact that I never want to see him again, so that I'm never, ever reminded of the kissing debacle, his thoughtfulness would be one more really great reason to be attracted to him.

Chapter 16

Now - Love and Hate

At breakfast I manage to eat a little something and down three cups of coffee. Everyone is quiet and reflective as we sit in the cafeteria waiting for time to tick by until day two of the emotional unloading begins. I'm trying to distract myself by sifting through my purse and organizing the chaos of receipts, gum wrappers, and sundry other items. I pull out a familiar and worn piece of paper. It's a journal entry from when I was a little girl. Sometimes I read it when I need a Callie fix. It makes me laugh and reminds me of the times we had together when we were small and had no idea what the future had in store for us. I have it memorized, but I like to take it out and touch the paper, it's like I can absorb some of my childhood through it.

Things I love about Callie
pritty
mermaid hair
tells me stories
makes good sanwitches
funny
likes kittens
does not think I am weerd
sticks up for me
braids hair good
nise
brave
her name

Things I hate about Callie
pritty
mermaid hair
bossy
older than me
lots of frens
she is taller
her name
makes me do dishes even when it is her turn
brakes my stuff when she is mad

You see, with Callie, the things I loved about her were often times the things I hated most about her.

Chapter 17

Now - Retreat Activity No. 4; Narrative Therapy

Before I know it, it's time to begin our first day of Narrative Therapy. As I leave the dining area, I feel as though I'm marching to my doom. Dead girl walking! I know I semi-committed myself to this process yesterday, but I'm having second thoughts now. I hate to feel weak and sappy in front of people. Clearly I don't mind falling apart at home while I'm fucked up and watching old, sad movies (*Beaches*, *Steele Magnolias*. Oh, how I wish Sally Field was my mother; it would be nice to have someone give me juice during a diabetic fit and mourn the loss of a child, like only Sally can). Occasionally I will fall apart at a bar, but I'm so drunk, I don't know that it happened until the next day when Luci is shaking her head at me while explaining how I lost my shit the night before. But today, today I must speak (soberly), divulge my secrets on purpose. Luci is right, I can't continue the way I have been and expect to have any kind of life that Callie could be proud of. I find Thomas, and we walk together toward whatever hell awaits us. He squeezes my hand when we arrive in the community room, and I'm grateful he doesn't start throwing words of encouragement at me – platitudes aren't what will help me now. Even though we have these pretend families, this is something that each of us must do alone.

I have no snarky thought or remark when Jodie asks if she can go first. I'm grateful. I'm not ready to speak yet. Terror at having to do this exercise has turned me mute.

Chapter 18

Now - Jodie's Story

"I've been looking so forward to this retreat, but now that I'm up here for this part of it, I'm actually nervous. You wouldn't know it to look at me now, but I used to be thin and kind of pretty in high school. I was even a cheerleader. I loved everything about cheerleading: the routines, cheering at games, and the sense of togetherness. I loved to decorate the athletes' lockers on game days and bake them cookies. I would package up the cookies with candies and make hand-written cards encouraging them to do their best. 'Go Big Blue! You can Do It! Go, Fight, Win!' I'd spend hours crafting beautiful signs for their lockers, it was really fun. On game days, I'd stand next to their freshly decorated lockers, so I could hand them their treats and secretly hope one of them would invite me to hang out after the game. I wasn't allowed to go out very much, but sometimes my parents let me go with the other kids to hang out at Burger King after a football or basketball game on Friday nights, if someone invited me. While I was with my classmates, I felt like I lived in a Disney movie; everything seemed perfect.

My home life was okay. I'm an only child, and my mom worked a lot while I was growing up. My dad was a junior high teacher, and when he came home from work, he'd help me with my homework, and we'd chat about our days. Sometimes he'd take me out and we'd split a pizza and have milkshakes – just the two of us. Those were my favorite nights. My dad coached his school's track team and ran the student newspaper;

the extra stuff took up a lot of his time. He was a really social guy, and I think he just wanted to be around people, and it also gave him a great excuse to not have to be around my mom very much. My mom was fine-ish back then, she just wasn't interested in me or my dad. I sort of wondered why she was even married to him. She was strict and conservative and told me no to almost everything I ever wanted to do or try. She wasn't a very happy person, and she didn't have patience for anything she thought was foolish or a waste of time. It was only a matter of time until my dad couldn't deal with her, and eventually they split up. Not too long after my parents divorced, my mom met someone, Larry. It was fine in the beginning because Larry wasn't around much since my mom worked so often. But over time, he did something to her; he put some kind of spell on her that turned her into a social butterfly. Maybe it's because he was a little younger than her, but he was able to charm smiles out of her and open up a social life that she seemed to really enjoy. My mom was suddenly this whole new person who wore her hair down and dressed in clothes she used to think were slutty when I would ask if she would buy them for me. Life for my mom revolved around Larry and his friends. I became almost non-existent, which had its up sides and down sides. I was able to go out with kids from school a lot more often, but I was also lonely. I missed my dad."

Up to this point, Jodie recites this story like she's practiced it for a pageant. I couldn't understand why she was here. So far it just sounds like she has standard "Daddy Issues."

"Larry moved in with us, and my mom stopped working so much so she could spend time with Larry and his friends. For a while, my dad still came around to take me out for pizza and milkshakes twice a week. I started to put on a little weight, but it wasn't too bad. I could still fit in my cheerleading uniform."

Her eyes are watering a bit now.

"After a while, my dad met someone – Lily. Lily, the drunken monster who tried to put me on a diet any time I was at their house. Lily has two perfect daughters from her first marriage who are thin and beautiful and completely socially acceptable. Pretty soon our twice weekly outings and our occasional weekends became once weekly outings and no weekends, and soon after that, they were once a month outings. Eventually the outings turned into holiday and birthday cards and a week in the summer where I followed the two perfect step-sisters around to all of their dance competitions. I had to watch my dad cheer them on with the emotion and gusto he used to have for me."

The tears are beginning to pour out of Jodie now but not sloppy tears, just streams of water glistening down her cheeks.

"I turned to food. I stuffed myself with the pizzas and milkshakes that my dad and I used to have together. I remember one time I went to the restaurant my dad used to take me to and told the waitress I was waiting for my dad to meet me, so that I didn't feel bad about ordering two milkshakes and a large pizza. I pretended not to notice the stares from staff and customers when I eventually pulled 'my dad's milkshake' in front of me and polished it off in minutes. I know they pitied me, but I just didn't care. It felt good to fill myself up until I thought I would burst. I never went back to that pizza shop after that, but I found plenty of other places where I could stuff my face. My favorite was the food court at the mall. I could eat my way around the entire food court and still feel hungry. I usually didn't get much attention from my mother, but after I gained about 50 pounds, I had more attention than I ever wanted from her. She yelled at me about how fat I was, and she would buy me bigger sized and out of style clothes from second-hand shops. She refused to spend much money on new clothes for me when I looked the way I did.

The small group of kids I counted as friends shied away from me at school. I didn't have a best friend I could trust to stick by me. I felt really alone. I was eventually shamed off of the cheerleading team and the invitations to hang out on Friday nights with kids from school stopped completely."

Jodie pauses to blow her nose, and her eyes go a bit vacant as she continues her story. I am a bitch and I'm starting to feel a little sorry for judging her harshly. I know how it is to feel alone.

"So one night my mom went out with the ladies, and Larry had his poker buddies over. They were drinking and smoking and who knows what. I was in my room trying to read *The Scarlet Letter*. I love to read, and I can get lost in a book for hours. After a while, I heard the front door close, and there was silence in the house. A few minutes later, I heard a knock on my bedroom door, and before I could answer, Larry walked into my room with a plateful of food. It was filled with things that I love to eat, but I said no, thanks. I felt uneasy as he sat on the side of my bed.

He began speaking to me softly, 'God, you really are beautiful. It doesn't matter what size you are, there is no hiding how gorgeous you are. I could drown in the blue of your eyes.' He brushed the hair from my face and tucked it behind my ear. His voice grew husky, and he continued to tell me which parts of me he liked best as he touched each part he named. He started with my hair, then my cheeks, my chin, my shoulders, and then my breasts. He used his thumbs to circle the nipple of each breast. I was ashamed because it felt good, and my body was responding. I let him do it. Then his mouth was on my mouth. I was nearly sixteen-years-old and I'd never been kissed, and it felt so good to have someone paying attention to me. Wanting me."

Jodie is crying harder now, but through deep gulps, she continues her story. I'm frozen in my seat; I know what must come next, and I feel sick...

"Nothing else happened that night. He left my room, and I curled up on my bed and replayed our encounter in my head. I felt beautiful, like one of the girls from *Gossip Girl*. Every time my mother was out, and Larry was left at home with me, we reenacted our first night together. He'd go a little further with me each time but not too far. Everything he did felt good and was at just the right speed. My birthday came around; it was my sweet sixteen. I got a card from my dad with $100 in it, and I was feeling pretty good that he remembered. Then surprisingly my mother actually planned for us to go to Chili's for dinner. It was just Chili's, but I was there with my secret boyfriend. I'd lost a few pounds without even trying, and my mother wasn't being a horrible bitch – I was feeling pretty great.

I remember ordering a salad for dinner, and it felt like it was enough for a change. I felt like enough. Mom and Larry had to practically force me to order a piece of cake for dessert. They sang Happy Birthday to me with just a little too much fervor; it was embarrassing. I sat eating my cake, and it was good, but I really didn't even want it. I didn't notice how much my mom had to drink until I looked in her eyes and realized she couldn't focus, and her left eye was practically shut. It was time to get her home; it made me miss the days when she worked a lot and had no social life. She passed out in the car before we even got home. I had to help Larry get her in the house and put her to bed. He thanked me for the help and then walked me to my room. He was a little more drunk than I was used to seeing him; not like he was going to pass out like my mom did, but he was slurring his words and he was staring at me like a starved lion stares at its prey. He sat on my bed and reached for me.

I remember saying, 'Larry, stop. My mom is here.' He shushed me and said she would be passed out for hours. I relented because I didn't know what else to do. Things felt wrong and not like the other times. He started shoving his hands up my skirt, and we had never gone that far before. He was rushing and he seemed angry and excited at the same time. I asked him to stop and he took a deep breath and told me to relax; he was just excited to give me my birthday gift. He leaned in and kissed me, but his breath was hot and sour, and his tongue was jabbing at the inside of my mouth. I was crying and begging him to stop, but instead he climbed on top of me and jammed himself inside of me. He didn't even take off my underwear…he just yanked it aside and did his thing. As he finished, all I could think about was how much it hurt and then I heard screaming. I thought it was me screaming, but I opened my eyes and there was my mother, standing in the hallway outside of my open door, screaming and calling me a whore. Larry jumped off of me and left to deal with my mom. I laid on the bed, not moving; my stretched-out underwear wet with blood and his gross stuff and my skirt still up around my waist. I must have fallen asleep that way because I woke up still half naked to my mother packing up my clothes. She was cursing at me and blaming me for seducing the man she loved. She would not have a fat whore living in her house. I was so confused. Larry hurt me; he took something I could never have back. I started to realize how awful the things he was doing with me for the last couple months really were. I was desperate for someone to hug me and tell me I'd be okay. Instead I was being cast out, shunned like Hester Prynne from the book I was reading. I thought I'd go live with my dad, but it turned out that he didn't have room in his house, or his life, for me. I had to go live with my grandmother, my mom's mom. Well, the apple doesn't fall far from the tree; she was as uptight and hateful as my mother. Living with my grandmother was nearly unbearable. The rest of high school was a pretty hollow existence for me."

I feel something give deep inside myself, and I'm looking at Jodie differently. I see how her experience was so similar to Callie's bad thing. Her cheerful gusto is a façade, and I wonder how often Callie faked her happiness. It makes me sad to think that maybe when I was having the time of my life with my sister, she was just playing along to please me.

Jodie has unfolded, and I see how she feels the need to please people and befriend them in hopes that they will like her for what she does for them. She doesn't feel that anyone could like (or love) her just for being herself. I feel sad and bad and all these things I don't want to feel toward her, but I do feel them. I've looked at Jodie like she is the complete antithesis of me, but now I see her similarities to Callie, and it softens me toward her. In many ways, she's just like me, too; Jodie has lived with guilt and abandonment for years – it came about differently than mine did, but she feels so many of the same things I do.

She walks back to her seat next to me, and without looking at her, I place my hand on her shoulder and give her a squeeze. It's the best I can do; I'm just not a big hugger. I go to move my hand away, and she grabs it and won't let go; we listen to Diego's story hand and hand (and shoulder).

Chapter 19

Now - Gibberish

DIEGO
Diego breaks my heart. Between his accent and deep sorrow, he isn't able to articulate much, just that he is a thirty-five-year-old father of two girls and the ghost of his four-year-old son. Through his sobs, we have learned that he had a beautiful, smart, vibrant-living son named Adrian, and now he does not. I recognize the guilt in his eyes. I can tell his story will be hard to hear once he's able to bring himself to tell it.

SILVIA
My heart is racing, and my mouth is dry. I'm next. My legs are boiled noodles as I try to stand. Jodie puts her hand on my back and reminds my body that it is a solid and not a liquid, and my legs make their way to the front of our small, pretend family. I feel like I'm having an out-of-body experience. I'm not sure I can do this. I try to remember how James helped ground me yesterday, but it isn't working. I hear a voice saying the name Callie, and I taste salt and copper. I hear the word "letter," and I feel dizzy. Something soft is in my hand; it's a tissue – how did it get there? I hear the name Scott, and that is when I realize it's me talking. I can't stop talking and crying. I can tell I don't make sense and I'm saying things out of order, but I can't stop. I'm talking and crying until I say the words out loud, the words that have chased me inside my head – they've finally caught me and push their way out of my mouth.

"It's my fault. I could have saved her."

I move without feeling my legs carry me back to my seat. I'm back inside my body now; I'm shaking and unfocused. It's Tammy's turn to purge, and I'm so grateful to not be the focus that I sigh loudly as I swallow down the sickness in my throat.

Chapter 20

Now - Tammy's Story

"I haven't faced the kinds of trauma that so many other people here have faced. I think, mostly, I'm just sad…and lonely. I never got married or had children. I have two French Bulldogs that I absolutely adore, Gus and Jacques. My mom moved in with me after my step-dad died, and she was with me for almost fifteen years. I thought it would be hard having her there; she was really outgoing and very mouthy. I've always been an introvert and quiet. I thought having her live with me would be suffocating, but it turned out we were the best kind of odd couple. We went to bingo nights at church, saw movies, took long, slow walks with Gus and Jacques, and had dinner twice a week at our favorite Greek restaurant; she'd call us the "Saganaki Sisters" because we always ordered that delicious flaming cheese at the restaurant. We lived like this for fourteen years, and we were both happy. There was nothing obvious that indicated my mom wasn't well; she was slowing down a bit and losing some weight, but nothing that made we worry too much. Time was passing, and she was getting older – I thought it was all normal. She was pretty good about seeing her internist for physicals, but she wasn't keeping up with her annual gynecological exams and mammograms. I tried to remind her a few times to make her appointments, and she'd always brush me off and tell me that she was all dried up down there and that she didn't need to go. She was so feisty. By the time she finally made her appointment and got her referral for her mammogram, she had stage IV breast cancer. At this point, surgery was not an option. The cancer had spread to her lungs and liver.

She had rounds of chemotherapy that just made her feel and look less like herself until one day she hugged me and held my face in her hands and said, "Sugar, I'm done with this shit. I love you as much as a mother can love a daughter, but I don't want to do this anymore." Hospice was brought in shortly after she stopped chemo treatments and then she died. There was no dramatic exit; she was there and then she was gone. There was an empty hospital bed sitting in my living room and nobody who needed it. I remember before the company came to pick up the bed, I noticed Jacques and Gus laying on it. I wondered if they knew something I didn't know, so I laid down on it to see if there was some of her spirit left, but there was nothing. It was just an empty bed. There were only six months between the time she was diagnosed and when she waved the white flag."

Tammy has a beautiful way of speaking. She tells her story without self-consciousness and draws you in with her unexpected smiles through her tears. I like Tammy; if I had a favorite aunt, I'd want her to be squishy and sweet like Tammy.

Chapter 21

Now - Thomas's Story

Last to go is Thomas. His tears flow before he even speaks, but they are stoic, brave tears that make you want to listen. He speaks in an even, quiet voice…

"I lost my partner Jeffrey when we were driving to Massachusetts to get married. We were so excited to be able to make a legal commitment to one another. It was a huge step forward for gay rights, and we were thrilled for the opportunity to exchange our vows. Our families weren't supportive of our "life-style," so we were on our own, but we had a lot of friends and they were our family. They still are my family. I was driving us down the Massachusetts turnpike; it was a beautiful day for driving. We were playing the alphabet game to pass the time. I can still remember that Jeffrey had the letter "C" and he found the word "cheese" on the side of the truck next to us. I thought it was so fitting since cheese was his favorite food; I teased him about eating so much cheese, he'd turn in to it, like I always did."

The way he smiles when he talks about Jeffrey gives me hope that maybe someone, someday will love me that way, and if I'm lucky, if I pull my shit together, I can love them back the same way.

"The traffic was terrible, but we were still moving along. There were some brake lights up to the right, but we were in the center lane and driving at a good clip. I strained to try to see past the truck in front of us, and that's when I heard Jeffrey yell. I turned and saw his wide, blue eyes full of fear. Then I saw what he saw – enormous tires moving toward us, or us toward them, I couldn't tell because it all happened so fast. I slammed on my brakes and looked for somewhere to swerve, but there was nowhere to go; we were boxed in by semi-trucks. I honked my horn and tried to move to my left, but there was no room. I heard the crunch of metal as the cheese truck to our right devoured the front passenger side of our car. We skidded for what seemed like forever and then we stopped. Our car was pinned under the semi. I thought, with some relief, that we must be okay. I looked at Jeffrey, he was alert and he was saying something. I was in shock. I couldn't hear his words and then I sensed movement outside of my window. My door opened, and people were trying to yank me from my car, but I wouldn't let go of Jeffrey's hand. I couldn't make sense of what was happening and why everyone seemed to be in a panic. Jeffrey was saying something, but his words weren't reaching me. The people outside of the car were pleading with me and finally managed to get me out, but I reached back in and screamed for Jeffrey to follow. It was then that the weird bubble in my head popped, and I could hear him.

'Thomas, I can't. I can't move!' For the first time, I looked away from his face and saw that the dashboard was crushing him and had him trapped. His door was caved in and pushing him askew. There was a lot of blood, but I couldn't tell from where it was coming. There were people breaking the windshield trying to get to him, but there was no way to reach him. The realization set in that even if we could get to him, there would be no way to extract him. We stared into each other's eyes for the last time; he understood he wasn't getting out of that car. The smell of gasoline started to penetrate the air. He told me it was okay, that I should go. He said he loved me. I wanted to stay with him. I sobbed and told him how much I loved him and then the people dragged me away, kicking and screaming. They took me to safety and kept me there. Agonizing minutes, maybe they were seconds, passed where Jeffrey sat in that car alone, waiting to die, and I couldn't do anything about it. I only hoped that the gas fumes or pain were too much and he passed out. I sat and watched with hundreds of strangers who were stuck on the expressway as my tiny vehicle exploded into flames, setting fire to the entire truckload of cheese. Charred cheese was everywhere. It was surreal. The smell of scorched cheese was mixing with the smell of gas fumes, and it was a nauseating assault on our senses. It was a sickening smell that I'll never forget. I wonder all the time about how much pain he was in. Jeffrey was the gentlest person I have ever known, and he died in such a horrible way."

I wasn't prepared for Thomas's story. Everyone in our pretend family is stunned into silence, and I can tell that his devastating story has taken the wind out of everyone.

I see a trend in all of our stories – guilt. What a truly powerful weapon it is.

Chapter 22

Now - Hairy Ass Guy

We've gotten through several rounds, and Tammy has stopped crying; she'll just be listening from now on. Jodie and Thomas have made a lot of progress today, so I don't expect they will need to speak for too long tomorrow. Diego and I haven't managed to say much of anything coherent, so tomorrow will be rough on us. I look around at the other groups, and everyone sort of looks like they want to throw up. The Loss Counselors look weary, like they consumed our stories to take the burden from us, like the guy from *The Green Mile*. I notice how Ben sort of hovers near our group during the last portion of narrative therapy, but he doesn't come over to chat. I think I might have really made him feel uncomfortable last night.

Dr. Wilson declares Narrative Therapy finished for the day, which is a total relief; today's exercise was like being wrung out and squeezed like a sponge, everything has been squished out of me.

My pretend family and I shamble back to our room like a pod of zombies, so we can rest and hang out before dinner. Tammy and the boys collapse on their cots while Jodie and I head off to the bathroom to freshen up. As we approach the women's locker room, we hear banging.

"What is that?" I ask.

"I'm not sure. It sounds like the noise the pipes in my house used to make when we showered, kind of a knocking sound," Jodie responds.

"Maybe that's it. I hope nobody is hurt in there."

We walk into the bathroom and find that the banging is louder inside. There's also a weird, muffled panting noise. Maybe someone is sick? Worried we head toward the back, where the showers are, and as soon as we round the corner, we are met by an enormous, hairy ass. This hairy ass is attached to a guy who has a random girl bent over and hanging on to the shower's handicap rail as he bones away.

"Holy shit!" I scream. I'm not a prude, but wow, it's like walking in on the set of a porno. I can't un-see his balls flopping back and forth, and I can't un-hear her moaning.

"Oh my God!" Hairy ass guy shouts.

"Oh, shit!" Girl I don't know yells as she covers herself with the shower curtain. She really needn't bother; we've seen all her goods from a very unflattering angle.

"I guess therapy is done for the day?" Hairy ass guy asks.

"Uh, yeah," I confirm.

The sex duo grabs their clothes and heads out of the locker room, and Jodie and I nearly fall to the floor laughing. We are absolutely hysterical, howling with laughter and hanging on to each other for dear life. The looks on the sex couple's faces were priceless. We pull ourselves together and head back to our room to share the story with the rest of the family.

We relay our story to the others, and the hysterics start all over. Thomas is laughing so hard, he begins to snort, and Tammy is sure she has peed her pants. Diego is laughing so hard, there is no actual laughter coming from him, he's just making strange "uh, uh, uh" noises. It feels so good to laugh; our overall exhaustion has fueled our maniacal laughter outbreak. I think we all needed to get some emotion out in some way other than tears.

Chapter 23

Now - Fireball

I walk over to my duffle bag and pull out my bottle of Fireball. I hold it up over my head, like baby Simba in the *Lion King*.

"Who wants to play 'I've never?'" Thomas and Jodie are enthusiastically shaking their heads yes, and Tammy and Diego look confused. "You'll love it! Just say yes," I coax. I unscrew the cap, and we all sit around in a circle on cots and bean bag chairs. "Just follow along, it's super easy. I will say something like, 'I've never had sex in the shower of a women's locker room!' And if anyone HAS had sex in the ladies' room, they take a drink. Easy peasy. I'll start. I've never been in a romantic same sex relationship!"

"That's a cheap shot!" Thomas scoffs but puts his hand out for the bottle. "My turn! I've never had a one-night stand…Come on now, come clean, guys…"

He doesn't have to ask me twice to come clean. I raise my hand and accept the bottle. Really, with the number of one night stands I've had, I should probably just down the entire bottle. The liquid cinnamon pours down my throat, and it is a welcome feeling as the warmth slides down into my stomach.

"Anyone else?"

In a surprise turn of events, Tammy raises her hand with a sheepish grin and accepts the bottle.

"Tammy, I am shocked and appalled! I thought so highly of you…" Thomas is laughing and feigning disgust.

"Tammy's turn!" Jodie yells.

"I don't know. Um, I've never been pulled over for speeding?"

Diego and Thomas both raise their hands and take their drinks. "Come on, Diego. Your turn," I insist.

"I've never swallowed the worm from a tequila bottle." He laughs as he sees Jodie raise her hand. He takes a swig and passes the bottle to her.

"What? Is that so hard to believe?" she asks. "Okay, I've never smoked pot."

I laugh because I'm faced with yet another "I've never" that should require me to drink the entire bottle, but then I look around and everyone has their hands raised, except Jodie.

"Tammy, I'm really starting to lose faith in you!" Thomas continues to tease her as he passes the bottle.

"My mom and I used to smoke it toward the end before she died. I like it." She giggles and gives Thomas a wink and hands him the Fireball.

"Okay. My turn, my turn," I say. "I've never roomed with four strangers and told them all my darkest secrets?" I give a sly smile, knowing I'm making all of us drink another shot. A collective groan goes up, but I can see that everyone is eager to take another swig.

We play a few more rounds until Tammy puts her hands up and refuses any more Fireball.

"I can't, I can't. No more. Please." She puts her head on her pillow and says, "I'll just rest my eyes for a minute. Just for a minute, don't let me sleep."

"Light weight!" Jodie teases.

We hear a snort and notice that Diego has passed out. Since the others seem to have run out of steam, Jodie, Thomas and I tip toe out into the hallway to give Tammy and Diego some quiet. We walk the halls until we find an empty room that isn't locked.

"Hey, look what I found!" Thomas is pointing to a radio. He reaches to turn it on, but the only station that comes in without any static is an oldies channel. Thomas grabs my hand and starts swinging me all over and twirling me around; I'm like a ragdoll in his arms. It's a good thing I have a nice buzz going because it allows me the freedom to dance without feeling dumb. The song changes to one I know well. I'm feeling the rhythm of "Don't Be Cruel" by Elvis Presley, and Thomas continues to throw me around while I giggle. He tries to push me through his legs and then swing me up, but I collapse to the floor like a giant potato and take him down with me. We start cracking up, and Jodie turns from the white board she's been drawing on to see us heaped on the floor in a tangle of arms and legs.

"Hey, that's really good!" Thomas exclaims as we both take in the intricate floral scene that Jodie has created. She has transformed a white board into a piece of botanical artwork; it's stunning.

"It's so pretty. Where'd you learn to do that?" I ask. I can only imagine how much better she could do when she isn't limited to just green, black, blue, and red whiteboard markers.

"I didn't really learn, I've always just doodled," she says.

"Jodie, my dear, you have a real talent," Thomas declares like he is a world-renowned art critic.

"Thanks, guys," Jodie blushes, but I can tell the praise has helped fill an empty spot within her.

Thomas and I untangle ourselves and walk over to Jodie, so we can examine her work more closely. It really is beautiful.

"Maybe we should head back and make sure Diego and Tammy wake up for dinner," I suggest. Thomas and Jodie agree, and we walk out of our little room. Jodie leaves her masterpiece for the next people who enter the room; maybe they'll find it after a hard day of narrative therapy, and it'll make them smile.

It's getting close to the end of dinner hours when we make it back to our room. Tammy and Diego are both sleeping peacefully. I almost feel bad waking them up. I gently shake Tammy's shoulder, but she doesn't move.

"Tammy? Do you want dinner? It's time to get up if you want dinner."

"Mmm, yeah, dinner," she mumbles.

"Okay then, it's time to get up." Tammy rolls over and cuddles deeper into her blanket.

"Tammy!" I say in almost a yell. "Wake up!"

"Okay, okay." Tammy opens her eyes and looks a little startled that we're all standing over her and staring at her. "Oh, hey. I must've fallen asleep."

"Ya think?" I ask sarcastically.

"I just need five minutes, then I'll be ready to go." Tammy heads off to the locker room.

Jodie has better luck with Diego; he's out of bed and stretching pretty quickly. After a few minutes, everyone is ready to get some chow, but my buzz is starting to wear off, and I'm starting to feel a little low again. The combination of today's therapy, Fireball, and laughing my ass off has completely drained me, and I'm not even a little hungry. Under protest of the others in my pretend family, I decide to skip dinner and go straight to bed.

Chapter 24

Now - Inner-Bitch

I am so tired, but I'm not sleepy. Focusing on the stories of others has given me a twisted kind of respite from the one I've been living the past eight years. I take this time alone in the family quarters to polish off the bottle of Fireball and welcome a black out.

I'm startled awake when I sense movement near me, and I realize Jodie is trying to get my attention. I must have been out for a while. My family members are all back from dinner and nestled in their cots, but Jodie is waving her hands at me like she's bringing in a Boeing-737.

"Silvia?" she whispers.

"Yeah?"

"Are you sleeping?"

"No, not now."

"I'm sorry," she appeals to me. "I saw Ben at dinner, and he wanted me to tell you hi from him. Isn't that nice? Oh, and I pointed out hairy ass guy and random girl to the rest of the family. I made eye contact with the girl and I thought she was going to jump out of her skin!"

"You woke me up to tell me that?" I admonish her, even though both things make me pretty darn happy to hear.

"Well, no, not exactly. I can't sleep," she explains.

"Well, yeah. It's hard to sleep when you're flapping your gums at me." Oops. My inner-bitch got out for a second. Better reel her back in…"What's going on?" I ask in much more caring-ish tone.

"I don't know. I just feel uneasy and I can't sleep."

"Why don't you try counting sheep?" I offer.

Jodie sounds dejected when she says, "Okay, I'll try."

I'm not great at being woken up, so I'm having a little trouble keeping the inner-bitch in check. I take a deep breath, shake myself awake, and try again, "Hey. I'm sorry. It was a hard day, and we opened a lot of cans of worms. Makes it hard to sleep for some of us."

"It's okay. I shouldn't have woken you up," Jodie whispers.

"Hey, it's scary saying out loud all the things we feel. I get it. I've carried my grief with me for so long; it's like a fucking merit badge or something. Who will I be if I'm not the girl who's all fucked up because her sister died? Maybe it's the only interesting thing about me, and if I let it go, I'll find I'm just some boring asshole, totally ordinary." It must be the Fireball that makes me chatty because I've just gone on a tangent about me instead of helping Jodie. I do that a lot, try to relate to others but turn it into something about me; it's a bad trait, totally selfish, and I add that to my mental list of things I need to work on.

"I don't think anyone would ever call you boring or ordinary... maybe an asshole though," Jodie pipes up.

"Did you just bust my balls?" A smile is spreading across my face. I like this Jodie. I can't help but giggle. Something inside me gives just a little bit more, and I can't help myself, I do like her.

I hear Jodie give a sleepy laugh, and she whispers good night.

"Hey, Jodes?"

I don't get a response from her; she's out like a light. I guess she just needed a little attention. I get it. I can see the shadow of trees towering outside our window, and as I watch them sway in the wind, a memory comes barreling at me. I'm wishing it away, but it won't listen and it makes impact:

"Shut up and jump, Baby Silvy!"

It didn't matter what I was afraid of, Callie's response to my fear was always the same: Shut up and do it. It didn't matter that we were climbing out of a second-story window and that I was terrified for my life. "Shut up and do it." Getting out of the window and onto the roof wasn't so bad; it was the two feet of nothingness between the roof and the tree we had to climb down that was the scary part. I had to get a running start, so I could jump far enough. Callie would go first – she didn't need a running start - and she would lean out of the tree and reach for me in case I didn't jump far enough. We had done it before, lots of times, but it was scary every time. I did it because I wanted this special, secret time with Callie, and I didn't want her to think I was a baby. We were only eleven months apart, but she was always calling me a baby. I wanted her to think I was brave, like her. Fighting through my fear was always worth it though. Once we were safely on the ground, we'd run to our back yard. Sometimes we'd go down to the creek that ran through our backyard to check on the polliwogs we'd caught and put in a jar, and other times we'd swing on our swing set or just sit in the garden, and Callie would tell me stories that she made up. Sometimes Callie would sneak a Heath bar from our mom's stash, and we'd savor it on our adventures in the dark. This time was different, we were going further. We were going to follow the creek south to the old cemetery. We didn't usually wander out of our yard during our secret, nighttime adventures, but this time was different. Callie had heard that if you leave a tape recorder in a cemetery over night that you can hear the dead talking on the recording. She was desperate to see if it would work. It wasn't terribly far from our house, but leaving the sightline of our yard felt like we were breaking a whole new set of rules.

 Earlier that day, we'd found an old tape recorder in the storage area of our basement, and that's what we left at the cemetery. We hid it in a bush with new batteries in it and the record button on. We headed home, and everything was going great on our way until I got my foot stuck in some mud near the edge of the creek just three houses down from ours. The thing about that creek is you had to be careful with your belongings because the creek was hungry. I'd lost at least five big Lip Smackers, a bracelet, my favorite Hello Kitty barrette, and my Barbie thermos in that creek. Once the creek gets a hold of it, it's best to just to kiss it goodbye. This time though, it was my good, school shoe. I was stupid to wear my good shoes, but when Callie came to get me, I just threw them on without thinking. I was desperately pulling on my shoe, begging for it to come free, and then it suddenly came loose with a gruesome suctioning sound. I wanted to celebrate, but before I could, I dropped my slippery shoe right into the creek. I reached for it and nearly caught it, but it disappeared into the deep part. My shoulders sagged with defeat, and I cried thinking about how much trouble I'd be in once my mom found out I lost my shoe. Callie told me to let it go and dragged me by my arm toward our house; we had to get home, so we wouldn't get caught.

"I can't let it go. Mom will be so mad in the morning, and she'll find out we've been sneaking out," I wailed.

"Shhh! No, she won't. Come on, Silvy! We'll think of something. I promise!"

We ran back to the house, and I cried myself to sleep knowing my mom was going to kill me in the morning.

I awoke the next day, and both of my shoes were in my room. I was confused but happy. Maybe I dreamt the whole shoe fiasco. As I rolled out of bed, I saw a very tired-looking Callie walk past my room on the way to the bathroom.

"Callie, did I dream everything last night? I thought I lost my shoe..."

"It wasn't a dream; you lost your shoe. I took a trip to the toilet bowl before Dad got home from work this morning."

The toilet bowl can be a little dangerous, but if you are desperate to retrieve your belongings and if they are large enough to not slip through, you can sometimes find them there, pushed against the grate.

"You went back out by yourself, Callie? That's crazy. Weren't you scared?"

My sister was the bravest person I knew, even braver than Luci. If something needed to be said or done, you could count on Callie.

"It wasn't so bad. I'd be more scared of Mom and Dad finding out we've been sneaking out at night," she explained.

I smiled at her and said, "You are the BEST sister in the whole world."

"Sisters for life," she replied while yawning.

God, I loved her extra in that moment. I loved her so much that I hardly noticed how soggy my shoe was when I slipped it on.

I try to focus on my sister's face in my mind for just a little bit longer, but the Fireball takes me away again to blissful nothingness.

DAY 3

Chapter 25

Now - Retreat Activity No. 4, part 2; Narrative Therapy

I wake up strangely worse and better at the same time. I know today is my day to get the whole story out in a way that doesn't require a decoder ring. I only hope I can do it with some dignity, but I'm guessing I will sound more like a tongue-twisted Porky Pig than Sally Field from *Steel Magnolias*. Maybe I could just belt out "Wind Beneath My Wings" like Bette Midler in *Beaches*…Or maybe, aliens will come down and abduct me; I'd prefer an anal probe to this torture.

Before I know it, it's time to get started. The last of us fumble through a few rounds and then break for lunch. During lunch I find myself alone with Jodie while the others are loading their trays. I'm too nervous to eat. I look at Jodie and try to see what I saw the first time I met her, but I don't see that Jodie anymore.

I must be looking at her funny because she asks, "What? What are you looking at? Is there food on my face? A booger?"

"No! No. Nothing like that. I just, I don't know. You're just different than I thought you'd be. I'm glad I met you. That's all." Ugh. Declarations like this gross me out, but it's true, and I just couldn't stop myself from saying it.

Shortly after lunch, we continue with our Narrative Therapy. Jodie makes it to the "no tears" phase, along with Thomas. Diego and I are both floundering but improving each time. I'm starting to see the light at the end, I just have this last hurdle to overcome.

Chapter 26

Now - Diego's Story

"I thought a lot last night about how to say what I need to say. There is no easy way, so I will just say it best as I can. I killed my mijo, Adrian. It was an accident but one I cannot forgive myself for. He was the baby, the last child my wife and I had before she passed away. I was supposed to watch over all my babies, I promised her I would, but I let her down. I let them all down.

It was a warm fall day, and my two girls were blowing bubbles in the front yard while Adrian was riding his Big Wheel on the sidewalk. He was driving crazy from side to side, trying to catch the bubbles. I was washing my car in the driveway and I would spray Adrian with the hose every time he pedaled past me; he screamed and laughed every time, like he wasn't expecting it, even though I'd done it twenty times. We were having such a beautiful day. I finished washing the outside of the car and decided to vacuum the inside, too. My car was really old, but I tried to take good care of it because a new one wasn't in our budget. Our driveway is on a steep incline, so I put the emergency brake on when I park. It's the kind of brake that is in between the two front seats and you pull the lever up to put it on and press a button while you push the lever down to take the emergency brake off. Well, at some point while I was vacuuming, I must have bumped the emergency brake button. I didn't notice that I did it. I walked to the trash can on the side of the house to throw out an old Happy Meal box, and that's when I heard screaming. I didn't notice at first because the kids were making so much noise but then I realized it was a woman's scream. I turned and saw what I *thought* had happened. I thought my car rolled down the driveway and ran into a lady's car and she was upset, which is what happened, but it was only part of it. I ran to the street where my car had smashed into the woman's car, so that the cars made a T. I wanted to calm the lady down and make sure she wasn't hurt, but then I realized why she was screaming. It wasn't just that my car had rolled down the driveway. My sweet boy was there, pinned between the cars. When my car rolled, he was pedaling by, and his Big Wheel became wedged beneath the bumper and the car pushed him until it hit the lady's car. I heard sirens, and the next thing I knew, the firemen and EMTs were working to get him from between the cars. He was very weak and suffered many internal injuries. Once the pressure from the car was removed from him, he went pretty fast.

I held his hand and I told him, 'Te quiero. Ve con Mama.' I love you. Go to Mama. Then he was gone."

Diego is a mess of tears and snot. Thomas puts his arm around him and tries to settle him a bit. He's whispering encouragement in Diego's ear, and Diego is nodding his head up and down. Dear God. Yesterday when I said that his story would be hard to hear, I didn't know how right I was. I don't know how a parent gets over something like that. I can't help but feel sympathy for what my parents must have gone through, even though they emotionally abandoned me once Callie was gone, they lost their first-born baby. My mind is swimming with the thought of what they must have gone through.

I must have grabbed on to Tammy's arm during Diego's story because her shirt is wadded up in my hand. She peels my hand from her forearm and she gives me an encouraging smile as she urges me to the front of our pretend family, so I can take my turn.

Chapter 27

Now - What Happened to Callie

"I had a sister named Calliope; we called her Callie. She was elven months older than me, and we were really close. Even though we were so close in age, Callie acted like she was much older and in charge of me. I let her think whatever she wanted, I just wanted to be close to her so I could soak up some of her light. Callie was really outgoing, smart, brave, and beautiful. I was a bit of an introvert, but with a little prodding from my sister, I was willing to try most things. There was no one else quite like Calliope Jane.

Callie was always a beautiful little girl, but as we got older, she blossomed into the most gorgeous young woman I'd ever seen, or have ever seen since. Her hair was every shade of blond and it was wavy, long, and perfect in every way. She had enormous, bright blue eyes framed by long, dark lashes. By the time she was fourteen, she was 5'8", thin, athletic, and had perfectly shaped size C boobs. I can't lie, I was jealous, but I also regarded her as a goddess. Me? I felt like a troll. My dull, dark blond hair couldn't decide if it was wavy, curly, or straight, so it was all three at once. My eyes were okay, gray-blue, but they didn't have the same sparkle that Callie's eyes had. I especially hated that I was short with acne, braces, and my boobs were barely a B at that point in my life.

Callie and I were really close growing up. Our parents were busy working most of the time, so we were on our own a lot.

When she was seventeen, Callie was attacked and raped by her boyfriend's best friend Scott. It was devastating for all the reasons you would think but also because her boyfriend, Gabe, chose to believe Scott's lies about having a secret relationship with my sister, that Scott didn't rape her, they were secretly seeing each other. From the events of one night, Callie lost her virginity, her boyfriend, her friends, and her dignity.

My best friend Luci and I spent hours devising plans to get her boyfriend Gabe to understand what really happened that night, to wake him from the spell that had him believing Scott's story. It was such bullshit; he wasn't even mad at Scott, but he had no problem blaming Callie for what he thought happened. I wanted to punch him and shake him and scream in his face until he snapped out of it. Since beating him senseless wasn't really an option, I attempted to approach him a few times during school, but he kept himself surrounded by friends, and there was never a time I could talk to him in private. I tried him at his house a few times, but after talking to me the first time I showed up, he wouldn't answer the door anymore.

When I'd try to talk to Callie about how she was feeling, she would brush me off. I wanted to help, and if she could just tell me what she needed, I would have done anything to help her. She promised she was fine. I knew she was lying, but I was seventeen-years-old and had no idea how to reach her when our sister bond failed me. She promised me that she was keeping her chin up and everything would blow over. I know she didn't want to tell our parents, but I was wavering. Maybe they could help. In the end, I decided not to go to them; I didn't want to break Callie's trust.

As prom neared, Callie seemed to perk up a bit. We spent some time together during spring break and shopped for her prom dress together. It felt more normal than it had for a while. We made plans to go to prom together, just us sisters. Prom wasn't necessarily my thing, but for my sister, I'd do just about anything. Callie seemed more at peace, and I remember feeling relieved. I thought we were moving forward and leaving that terrible night far behind. About a week before prom, she handed me a beautiful envelope with my name written on it in looping letters and hearts dotting the i's in my name.

She said, "If anything should happen to me, read this." I thought it was strange, but I went ahead and hid it in my underwear drawer anyway. For a couple of days after she gave it to me, I had to keep myself from opening it but then I got busy with a school project and forgot all about it.

The night of prom arrived in mid-May. It was a gorgeous night; it was warm, and you could smell all the new plants, trees, and blossoms that had recently sprouted. I was wearing my necklace that I had bought on our prom dress shopping trip and was excited to present Callie with the near-matching one. When I gave it to her, she choked up a bit and hugged me hard; she held me for a long time. She put her matching necklace on and held the charm for a moment, like she was making a wish. She sniffed, smiled, and then pulled my hand, so I'd follow her to her bedroom. Callie and I got ready together in her room with the windows open. I borrowed a black dress from her closet, and she glammed it up with all the right accessories. She spent an hour curling and pinning my hair just so; it was spectacular. I let her do my make-up, glittery shadow, thick black liner, shimmering powder, sticky gloss. How did I never notice just how much we really did look alike? For the first time, I felt truly beautiful standing next to her. She moved behind me, and we stood looking in the mirror. She was wearing a robe with her hair and make-up done. She rested her chin on my shoulder and pulled out her phone to take a selfie of us. Anyone who saw that picture of the two beautiful, smiling girls wouldn't have guessed that only one of the two of us would be alive by the end of the night. We looked like we belonged on the cover *Teen Magazine*.

Once Callie was done putting her finishing touches on me, she demanded I pose for pictures. She started shouting all kinds of directions, like she was a professional photographer: Make love to the camera, work it, girl, booty tooch, find your angles…I smiled, pouted, growled, and bent every which way. We laughed like maniacs until we were out of breath. Callie hugged me hard and told me she loved me. She was staring fiercely into my eyes; it made me a little uncomfortable. I looked at her like she had two heads, but her weirdness was worth the extra helping of attention from her. After a minute, she kicked me out of her room, so she could finish getting ready; she said my beauty was a distraction and she needed to concentrate if she was going to make herself so gorgeous that she'd knock everyone dead at prom. I rolled my eyes at her, but I left and went to sit downstairs with my parents. My dad whistled as I came down the stairs. I remember that because it's the last time I can remember him really seeing me and thinking I was beautiful. We sat waiting, and after almost an hour, my mom sent me upstairs to check on Callie; she was worried we'd be late for the dinner portion of the evening. I climbed the stairs while thinking about how to handle the situation if someone started to give Callie a hard time; I liked to think of exit strategies and come back lines ahead of time since I got too nervous to think on my feet sometimes. I was snapped out of my thoughts when I got to the top of the stairs and slipped. I nearly tumbled backward and down the stairs. My heart was thumping at my near-death experience, but once my breathing returned to normal, my brain clicked on and I wondered where the water came from. I looked down and a found a rivulet of water coming down the hallway from the bathroom. My heart started to race again as I walked further down the hallway. I wondered if Callie slipped and fell and hurt herself. I called for her, but I didn't get an answer. I walked to the bathroom door, still calling her name, and stopped short when the door opened with barely a tap; that was weird. I walked in, and the water around my feet sloshed. I looked around the corner at the tub and saw her there, eyes mostly closed, body lifeless, submerged in red liquid.

I don't remember if I called for my parents or if I screamed when I saw her, but at some point, my parents had made their way upstairs and were standing next to me, crying and screaming, "No!" My dad found the soundness of mind to tell my mom to call 9-1-1. I remember that. And I remember him trying to get me to leave the bathroom and me refusing but then things got blurry.

I don't remember sitting down on the bathroom floor in the pink water, but that was the next thing I realized when I snapped out of my initial shock. I was holding her hand and staring at her heart necklace through the red water in the tub; I couldn't look at her face. She looked like Callie but not. Without her life-giving blood pumping through her body, she looked like a poorly painted porcelain doll. She was so white compared to the red in the tub. People sloshed into the bathroom, and I yelled at them to leave; she wasn't decent. I knew she wouldn't want strangers to see her that way. The people gave me sorrowful looks and pushed past me anyway. I saw a man taking pictures, and I wanted to kick him and make him stop. A woman was placing lettered signs on the floor and tub. Men lifted my sister from the bloody water and placed her on the ground. Her arms were slack, and her head lolled toward me. I noticed her eye make-up was barely on, and it was sort of smudgy. Was she crying when she did it? I could picture her crying and then snapping out of it, wiping at her eyes and then getting to work opening her veins. I watched as the people continued to work. They never made me leave, they were too busy dancing a dance they must have done before; they were good at it. They moved around each other effortlessly in the tight space. EMTs checked for signs of life, they even did CPR for a couple minutes, but I knew she was already dead and so did they. Her light had gone out. The man took more photographs, and the woman pulled a knife I'd never seen before from the tub. The knife in any other setting would seem innocuous. How could something so small wreak such havoc? My dad was hugging my mother in the hallway while they both cried and begged the EMTs to save their daughter. There was no saving her though.

I felt detached from my body. The sounds of paramedics working and my parents wailing was gone. I don't know how much later it was, but the EMTs left, and we were instructed to wait for the coroner's vehicle. I knew she was gone, but I hated that they left her there on the floor without a blanket or pillow. I yanked a towel down from the rack above me and spread it over her nakedness. It didn't seem right to leave her exposed. When the coroner finally arrived and two men came in to take my sister away, I lost my mind. I sobbed uncontrollably and screamed at them not to take her. I begged and pleaded until my dad coaxed me to my bedroom and sat me on my bed. I was a little girl again, looking up at my daddy, hoping he could fix what was broken, but of course he couldn't. He hugged me anyway and let me cry into his soft shirt like I used to. It was the last time I ever did that. Pretty soon my mom came up to get my dad, so they could go to the morgue and the police station. I couldn't stand to go with them, and they asked if I wanted my Nonna to come over and stay with me. I shook my head no, and they agreed to let me stay home if Luci came over.

A short time later, Luci arrived and my parents left. Standing in that house, knowing Callie would never be in it again, seemed impossible.

'She can't be gone. She won't breathe ever again. She won't smile ever again. There will be no more Callie. No more sister for life. This can't be happening. They will come home and tell me it was a mistake. She's alive. They have to, right? They have to.'

Luci stood there crying as I begged her to tell me that this was all a mistake. She didn't know what to do with such raw grief. It wasn't very fair of me to ask her to come over to deal with it with me. How could two seventeen-year-old girls figure out how to handle something of this magnitude? Eventually she came to me and hugged me. I couldn't hug back; I stood there and just let her hug me. As she squeezed, I could feel my spirit leave me; it left me hollow, like an empty husk. This is how I would handle everything, stay hollow, don't feel it. After a minute, I put my hands on her shoulders and gently pushed her back to let her know I was done being hugged.

She took my hand and said, 'Come on, Sil. Let's get you cleaned up and changed.' We went up to my bedroom and she helped me change into some sweatpants and a t-shirt. She sat me down and removed my make-up with a wipe. I was so far away that I could barely feel the cool, wet cloth on my skin. Luci unpinned my hair and kneeled behind me on my bed to brush my hair. It was soothing, and I let her keep brushing it for a while. When she finished brushing, she braided it and placed it on my shoulder. We laid in my bed, took out my tablet, and turned on Netflix. I don't know what she put on; I wasn't really watching. I liked the noise though. It was too quiet in my house.

Hours later I heard a car in the driveway, so I headed downstairs. My parents were home, but Callie wasn't with them. Most of me knew she wouldn't be, but part of me had still been hoping. My mom sat at the kitchen table and took a clear baggy out of her purse. She set the baggy on the table, and I recognized the contents as the jewelry and hair clips that Callie was wearing. My mom spilled the contents onto the table and slipped a bracelet on her wrist. She sat there, touching the bracelet and staring at it. I walked to the table and picked up the rose gold necklace with the crystal heart that I'd given to Callie just hours before. I touched the duplicate necklace that hung around my neck and turned and went upstairs to lay back in bed with Luci. When I got up there, instead of laying down, I rooted around for a small box. Once I found one, I placed Callie's necklace in it and then removed mine from around my neck and put it in the box next to Callie's. Two hearts in a box. It seemed fitting since I'd be burying my heart with hers in a bigger box in a few days. I climbed back into bed next to Luci and fell asleep to the sounds of laughter on Netflix.

I had the most magical dreams of Callie that night. I couldn't remember what they were about, but while I dreamed them, it felt like I could feel her light shining on me again. I hated to wake up, so I stayed in bed for days trying to re-create the dream, but it never came back to me. I don't even know when Luci left, but she was gone, and I was alone. I had to get out of bed on the third day for Callie's wake. I wouldn't go in our bathroom, so I showered in my parents' room and dressed myself in a black romper and my Chuck Taylors. I didn't bother with my hair or the little bit of make-up I usually wore.

We had the wake, followed by the funeral the next day. Someone had done Callie's hair, and it didn't look quite right; they painted color back into her skin and had taken their time applying way too much make-up. The one thing that was right was that she was wearing the dress that we'd bought her for prom.

The day was what you'd imagine it was: shocked family and friends repeating colloquialisms that people say to each other when they are grieving – sorry for your loss, in a better place, far too young to die, time will heal you…I let my relatives hug me and I thanked them for coming. Kids from school showed up, and I wondered how some of them could even show their faces at Callie's funeral. Did they think this was some kind of show? Or did they actually care? My bet was some of them were there for popularity reasons, so they could gossip about the funeral at school, make my sister's death about themselves. I could pick out faces that just a month ago were calling my sister a slut. I was still hollow, so I didn't feel anger then, but it was simmering where I couldn't see it. I was most surprised and angry to see Callie's former friend Sarah there. Did she want to paint the word "slut" on her coffin like she did on her locker? I was toying with the idea of going over and demanding that she leave, make such a big scene that she'd feel shame like Callie did. But before I could muster up the anger with which to do it, I deflated back into a husk. Sarah caught my eye and gave me a small wave. I think I saw regret there, but I refused to give her the benefit of the doubt. She never did that for Callie; in fact she was one of the kids that fueled the hatred toward my sister. I turned my back on her and continued hugging family and friends until it was over. I didn't expect it, but leaving that funeral was hard. We put Callie in a box and put the box on a shelf like a toy we were done playing with, except I'd never get to play with her again.

After the funeral, we headed to a restaurant where I endured as much as possible until I couldn't take it any longer and asked Luci to drive me home.

When we got to my house, Luci helped me go through Callie's room. I was afraid my parents would box up all her things and donate them one day and I wouldn't have a chance to take what I needed to survive without her. We went through her clothes and took what meant the most to me. I offered a few things to Luci, but she wouldn't take anything. I tried to explain that she was a second sister to Callie and that she'd want her to have something, but she still refused. I grabbed Callie's laptop, her journal, and her jewelry. I looked around to see what else called to me and decided I needed her pillow, blanket, and Mr. Owl-y. Mr. Owl-y was a stuffed owl made out of mink that Callie carried everywhere as a kid. She loved it so hard that she loved the face right off it, and now it just looked like a fuzzy, brown number eight. We dumped everything in a pile on my floor, and it struck me that all I had left of my sister was in a pile at my feet. We placed Mr. Owl-y and her blanket and pillow on my bed, Luci folded and hung clothes for me, and I put away the jewelry. I needed to hide her journal somewhere, so I put it where I put all my stuff that needs hiding – my underwear drawer. I opened the drawer and slid the journal in but noticed an envelope I'd forgotten about. I picked up the envelope and traced my finger over Callie's writing. My hollowness started to fill with grief, and I couldn't fight it off. Tears slid out of my eyes. The letter…"If anything should happen…" I opened it carefully, so I didn't ruin the beautiful letters on the outside of the envelope.

Dear Silvy,

I'm sorry I've been such a burden to you recently, and I'm sorry to burden you with this decision I've made, but if anyone can understand, it's you. You are the one bright spot in my life, and I wish that could be enough for me. I'm so empty inside that not even the best sister in the world can fill me back up.

Times with you have been the happiest in my life – playing, talking late into the night, fighting, camping, watching old movies, catching polliwogs, climbing trees, sneaking out of the house…Our trip around Michigan to find my prom dress…I will miss those things, and I hope we have made enough memories to keep me alive in your heart. You are so special, and a part of me will always be with you. Please know how smart, kind, and beautiful you are. I wish you could see yourself as I see you.

People say words have power. But they don't have the power to un-do what has already been done; they can't reverse time. There isn't a sorry big enough to make things right. Even when I'm smiling or laughing, one word chases me. Slut. That word had power; it made people believe the worst in me. I wish the word "No" would've had the power to stop Scott that night and then later when he spread his lies about me. God, I hate him.

I log into my apps at night and see what the kids call me. Slut. That word won't leave me alone. It was so easy for everyone to decide it's me who is a slut and not Scott who is a piece of shit. I've noticed a few people who look like they want to believe me, but they don't say anything to me. I wonder if they understand what their silence has helped me to decide. I doubt it.

I hate that people don't understand me, that they don't know me well enough to understand that I wouldn't lie about what happened to me. What did I do to make people want to hate me?

I need you to do one last thing for me, Sil. I need you to tell Mom and Dad that I'm sorry. I know they won't understand. Please tell them that I'm sorry I'm not who they thought I was. I tried to be her, but she didn't fit right, and now I'm so tired of trying to be her; I just can't anymore. I love them so much for trying so hard to be good parents.

All of this pretending is exhausting. I'm done with it. You are so strong, Sil. One day you'll see you are better off without me. I love you so much.

Sisters for life,
Calliope
xoxo

I remember after I read the letter, I crumpled to the floor in a heap and cried more tears than I thought humanly possible. My rage that had been simmering under the surface since the night I found her in the tub spewed forth from me in a screaming fit as I up-ended chairs and swiped surfaces clean of anything on them. If I would have opened that letter when she gave it to me, maybe I could have saved her, at least I could have tried.

Now that I'm grown, I know something inside of her was broken, and her suicide wasn't my fault, but had I understood what those words meant, "If anything should happen..." maybe I could have gotten her some help. Those words haunt me every. Fucking. Day. Reading that letter was the moment I became angry with Callie. She left me. For what? Did she think people would feel bad? If you kill yourself, you don't get to experience people feeling bad about your death or sorry for how they treated you; you don't experience anything. You're dead.

I never shared Callie's letter with my parents. Maybe it was cruel not to, but I felt so guilty that I thought they'd be angry with me. Plus it felt like my last sister secret with Callie, and I wanted to keep it for myself. It turned out that it didn't matter anyway, my dad retreated inside of himself and took up drinking like it was an Olympic sport. My mom joined a church grief group and befriended a widower that she later had an affair with. My dad didn't really notice, and when she finally asked him for a divorce, he didn't put up a fight. There was no war waged over me or any belongings; they had both simply given up on what was left of our family. It was the summer after my junior year when my mom left, so I didn't have much time before I would be leaving for college. I decided to stay with my dad for the rest of high school because he kept the house. I wasn't ready to leave the place where Callie's memory was strongest, and I certainly didn't want to have to put effort into getting to know my mom's new boyfriend. I got through my senior year because Luci was by my side. She was determined to keep me safe for the rest of our time in high school. You see, Callie's fire may have gone out, but Luci's fire was raging.

Once we graduated high school, Luci and I left for college, but I just used it for an outlet to party. I finally quit school after three years of wasting everyone's time and money. I got a bartending job and moved into an apartment with Luci, who was still in school. We still live together now, well, at least I hope we do. She's the one who encouraged, or threatened, me to come to this retreat. I guess I've hit rock bottom, as they say, and I think it's hard for her to keep cleaning up my messes. I'm still stuck in the past living the time of my sister's suicide, and she's ready to grow up and move on."

I walk back to my seat feeling relieved and completely dry-eyed. I've actually done it. My pretend family envelops me in a hug when I get to them, and I feel so proud of each of us for getting through this.

Chapter 28

Now - Letting Go

The feelings that began blossoming in my chest a couple days ago have grown, and when I look at the faces of my pretend family, there really isn't anything pretend about them. They are my new family, and saying goodbye to them tomorrow is going to be difficult. I don't know what's going on with me right now, but I'm feeling really emotional about leaving, and I'd really like to do something nice for them. The desire is overwhelming, and I know I need to do something to show them how special they are to me. I would love to buy them each a gift, but there aren't any gift stores in this facility. I'm not interested in writing everyone a letter, and I can't just take them to dinner since meals are included with the registration fee and there are no restaurants here. I think for a few minutes and then an idea begins to form in my head. I ask my new family to meet me in the courtyard later. I'm met with questions and strange looks, but I just smile at them and tell them it's not a huge deal, I just want to spend some time with them before we go (which is true).

    I part ways with the others and I run to the café to find all the most normal snack foods I can and buy drinks from the vending machine. My arms are loaded with snacks, drinks, napkins, and plastic forks. I run down the hall dropping napkins and silverware as I go. I wish I had a bag. This next part is the hardest. I arrive at my destination and knock on the door. Ben answers with a surprised look on his face that morphs into a smile that shows off that sexy dimple. Damn.

"Hi," I say, feeling really unsure of whether or not I should be there.

"Hi back." God, he is so cute!

"Can you help me with something? I didn't know who else to ask, and you did mention you hoped we'd chat again before the retreat is over so…"

"What do you have in mind? A bag? You seem to be overloaded," he asks as he opens the door and ushers me into his room. Ben finds a plastic grocery bag, and I deposit my items in it. I spend the next few minutes explaining my plans while trying not to get lost in his big, brown eyes.

"What I'd really like you to help me with is getting your hands on the helium tank and balloons that they used for the cocktail-dinner party the other night. I'm going to hunt down some sharpie markers and index cards. Can you meet me by the gazebo in twenty minutes?" He agrees, and we go our separate ways. I drop off the supplies that I've gathered so far at the gazebo, then I search inside the building looking in rooms to see if I can find any office supplies. I hit the jackpot in the third place I look and I find sharpie markers. I don't see any index cards, but there is computer paper and a scissor, so I opt to take those and get over to the gazebo to start setting up.

When Ben arrives, he has brought a few extra items that were in the supply room: a bottle of champagne, a tablecloth, and plastic champagne flutes.

"I wasn't sure if I should bring the champagne; think you can control yourself around me?" Ben teases me, and I feel my face heat up and my stomach drop. I'm so embarrassed. Are you there, God? It's me, Asshole. Beam me up please.

"Um, yeah. About that…" I start.

"I'm just messing with you! I was flattered, and if we were anywhere else, I would have kissed you so hard." Okay, could my face get any hotter? I might pass out. He really likes to hit things head on. It's pretty uncomfortable for someone like me who'd prefer to sweep it under the rug and then just move on. "Seriously I was just kidding with you. Don't be embarrassed."

I stand there like an idiot. I'm unsure what to do, but Ben saves me when he offers to pick some flowers for me, so we can put them on the table. He comes back with my favorite, blue hydrangeas; we probably weren't supposed to pick them, but I don't think anyone important will notice. He helps me finish setting up the table with the tablecloth, flowers, and all the snacks I dragged over here. We notice some twinkle lights on a tree near the building and we sneak over, laughing as he lifts me up, so I can steal them for my party. We add them to the gazebo; they are the perfect finishing touch to our surprise party. I'm so giddy with anticipation, I can hardly keep myself together, or it could just be the affect that Ben has on me. We fill the balloons with helium and twist the ribbons around a rock, so they don't float away. Now that we've finished, there is nothing left to do but wait. We sit in the grass next to each other and watch as the sun sinks away to nothingness. We chat for a while about the rest of my new family, and in the glow of the twinkle lights, I can see out of the corner of my eye that Ben is looking at me, and it makes me excited and uncomfortable at the same time. Total silence when I'm alone with someone makes me start babbling nonsense.

Before the babbling can start, I say, "Thank you so much for your help. I really couldn't have done this without you."

"Are you kidding? It's the most fun I've had in days. Thank you for letting me be a part of it," he replies.

"Will you stay with us? I'd love it if you would. Maybe you could tell us your story?" I don't know where all this bravery has come from, but it pays off when he says he'll stay.

My new family arrives all together, and Ben and I yell surprise as they walk up to the gazebo. I have a quick flash of the surprise parties Callie and I used to have for our parents, and my heart flutters for a second. It passes quickly, and I smile at the little group that has become like real family to me.

"What's all this? It's beautiful," Tammy asks smiling.

"It's our last night together, and I wanted to do something special for you. I had a rough start here, but you guys and this process have helped me realize and overcome so much. It's the least I could do… literally there is nothing else in this place that I could have used to create this surprise," I respond laughing. My family laughs, and I clear my throat and continue, "I did plan a couple little activities, but I had some help from Ben with the most important part. Everyone knows Ben, right? He's going to join us for the rest of the night, if nobody objects. He has had the chance to hear our stories and personal information, so he has agreed to share his." They nod their heads, and they look unsure about why I've asked them here. They're probably worried that, knowing me, my planned activities will include shots of Fireball. "Well, let's get started, then." We all sit, and I notice how different everyone looks compared to our first day. There are more smiles, there's more chatter, and everyone seems to be glowing a little. It feels like some weight has been lifted from us. Looking at each person, I think about how much I want them to remain in my life after tomorrow and I hope they feel the same way. I have a history of bad goodbyes, so maybe starting tomorrow I can change that. It seems like a reasonable first step toward my new lease on life.

Ben stands and begins to speak, "Hey, guys. Thanks for letting me join your group tonight." Ben smiles, I swoon, and then he continues, "I've had a lot of practice telling my story, so I'll keep it short. When I was younger, I was a partier. I mean frat boy, keg-stands, flippy cup, beer pong, suck and blow, you name it. I still can't believe I didn't die from alcohol poisoning in college. The night of my graduation, some of my fraternity brothers and I threw a party to celebrate. It was out of control. There must have been a hundred drunken people dancing, playing games, and making out. To make a long story short, I had way too much to drink and thought I was invincible. I climbed onto the roof of our fraternity house and jumped off like I was the Incredible Hulk. My left leg basically exploded on contact with the ground. The rest of my body was a mangled mess, too, but my leg looked like it went through a meat grinder; at least that's what all my buddies told me later. The fact that I was even alive after that jump was a miracle all on its own.

I eventually woke up in the hospital with only hazy memories of what had happened. My parents were there, and they looked so sad. My dad came over to my bedside and explained, in detail, how I nearly killed myself. The list of damages I'd done to myself was extensive and incredibly serious. In the end, while the doctors tried to keep me alive, I suffered a lot of complications, and they ended up having to remove my leg from the knee down."

At this point, Ben leans over and lifts his pants to show us his prosthetic leg. I am shocked. I was expecting a story like mine or someone else's in the new family, but I guess loss comes in many forms.

"I spent a long time being angry and battling depression. It wasn't until I started seeing Dr. Wilson two years later, when I was twenty-three, that I began dealing with my issues about the loss of my leg. I eventually worked through my anger and sadness; it's a work-in-progress though. I will battle those demons for the rest of my life. I did therapy with Dr. Wilson for three years, I attended one of these retreats, and then she eventually helped me put my psychology degree to use as a grief counselor in her practice. Now I'm back in school again to get my doctorate. That about sums up how I got here."

I can't believe how amazing he his. He's been through so much and he is really a wonderful man, strong, selfless, funny…and sexy as hell.

Everyone smiles at Ben and thanks him for sharing. I stand back up and start to instruct the others on our first activity, "You'll notice pieces of paper and pens in front of you. I thought it would be nice if each of us wrote our contact information, a quick note, or a couple of words to each person, whatever you want. Something we can take home and reach for when we need a little help getting through the day." We all spend a little time writing and then passing the notes out to each other. Instead of reading them now, we all shove them in our pockets, like it was part of the plan. I stand up and hand markers to each person and then pass them each a balloon. "Since we have to say goodbye to each other tomorrow, I thought it would be fitting to say goodbye to some of the baggage we brought here with us. Honestly I know with the amount of baggage I brought, I could fill a dozen balloons. But think of all the words you want to let go of and write them on your balloon: Guilt. Hate. Anger. Loss. Fat. Alone. Scared. Stupid. Old. Empty. Bitch. Slut. Once we're finished writing on them, we can let them float away."

After we spend some time filling our balloons with painful words, we walk out from under the gazebo to release our finished products into the night sky. I go first, and although I have many words on my balloon, I choose just one and scream it into the night as I let go of the string, "SLUT!"

The rest of my new family members follow one at a time:
Jodie – "FATASS!"
Diego – "MURDERER!"
Tammy – "LONER!"

Ben – "GIMP!"
Thomas – "FAG!"

We are silent for a few minutes while we watch our balloons fly away and take some of our sadness with them.

"That's that, I guess. I sure hope these balloons don't land at a preschool," I say to break the silence and then I move toward the gazebo; everyone follows me and takes a seat. Ben is helping me pour glasses of champagne, and when we finish pouring, I stand to make a toast.

"I can't believe the difference three days can make, but I feel a little more like myself than I have in a very, very long time. Not to sound trite, but I really couldn't have done this without all of you. From the morning of the first day, I referred to all of you as, now don't be mad at me, my 'pretend family.' Today, standing here, I know you aren't pretend; you are my NEW family. I hope you feel the same way and I hope we can all stay in touch. We have been brave in this battle against ourselves, and I'm so proud of us. We are warriors. Here's to continuing our journeys in the right the direction. Salute!"

"Salute!" everyone responds.

We sit around chatting for a little while, but we all know that we need to start packing and get some rest for our last morning together, so everyone cuts out pretty quickly. Ben lingers and helps me clean up, even though there isn't much to do. Once we toss everything in the trash and fold the tablecloth, Ben hands me the flowers and tells me I should keep them. I take them from him and tell him that they're my favorite kind. He smiles, so I can see that sexy dimple, and then he walks me back to my room. It isn't a ground-breaking moment, but it's a nice moment, and sometimes nice is enough.

Ben offers to return our supplies, and I head off to bed. As I'm falling asleep, I realize that I hardly drank anything tonight. I don't even feel like I need it to fall asleep. I'm exhausted.

DAY 4

Chapter 29

Now - Packing Up

It's our last morning waking up in our cotton ball room; I'm going to miss it. I pack the last few things into my duffle, flatten my flowers from Ben between the pages of my registration packet, and zip my bag. I look around and notice the others are also finishing up.

"Should we get this show on the road?" Thomas asks. He takes my hand, and we all walk to the community room together one last time.

There is a beautiful fruit and yogurt bar set up for breakfast. We set our bags down against the wall with all the other bags and head to the breakfast bar. We pile fruit and Greek yogurt into our bowls and eat it standing up while we walk around and say goodbye to everyone. I run into Ben, and I thank him again for helping me set up the surprise party last night. He's on the clock, so he keeps our conversation short and sweet, but we manage a short conversation that leaves me a little unsatisfied. What I really want to do is jump into his arms, wrap my legs around his waist, and kiss him until he's blue in the face. Yeah, that'd be good.

Chapter 30

Now - Retreat Activity No. 5; Meditation

"Good morning, families." Dr. Wilson is smiling, and she looks different to me today, less business-like and more approachable. She's wearing yoga pants and her hair is in a messy bun on top of her head, like mine. There are four neat rows of yoga mats laying out; each row is a different color. She instructs us to claim a row for our families. We walk to the row of kiwi-green mats and wait for directions.

"Please take a seat on your mat, sit however you are most comfortable. If you prefer to lay, that's fine, too. This meditation is whatever you want it to be today."

Everyone sits or lays. Soft music begins, and Dr. Wilson continues softly, like she's trying to put toddlers to bed, "Start by closing your eyes and just breathing, in through your nose and out through your mouth. Inhale for a six count, if you can, hold it for four and exhale for eight, or for as long as you can. That's right. Keep breathing, slow and steady. Good. While you continue to breathe, picture yourself sitting on a beach. You are comfortable, and the sand isn't sticking to you; it's warm and soft. Clear, blue water is in front of you, and there are waves lapping at the shore. You are breathing. In through your nose and out through your mouth. You can hear birds and the water, but otherwise it is quiet. You feel warm and content sitting quietly, breathing."

I'm reflecting on what brought me here. I'm not sure if that is proper meditation, but it's what is happening. I don't expect my sadness and anger to disappear because of one retreat, but I feel like my anger has been diluted, and my sadness has been locked down in a compartment where I can take out parts when I choose to work on them. If the things we've done here can help keep me from being the emotional nightmare I was over the years, then I'm going to follow up and find a therapist. I really like this taste of the old me, and I'd like to continue to see more of her. I know this is just a little sample of how good I can feel, and I can't wait to feel how light I'll be in a few months if I keep battling. Life is worth the hard work. I wish Callie would have given herself the chance to feel this way. If she could have understood that there is no greatness in dying, only in living and persevering, she would have had an opportunity to taste this emotional freedom.

I can hear Dr. Wilson now, "You are feeling refreshed. The beach is starting to fill with people, all the people you've met over the last few days. The sun turns to electric lights and the water into windows. You are in the community room. Open your eyes and see the others around you."

The music turns off, and everyone eventually stands. After a few more goodbyes, we all walk over to grab our bags and turn to leave the facility. The staff is at the door wishing us luck and watching us walk out single file. I turn and wave at Ben, and he gives me a wink. Maybe that's something…I look down the line of cars and see Luci a few cars down. I give some quick, final hugs to my new family and then I take off at a sprint and hop in Luci's car. She has a look on her face like she's not sure if I'm going to kill her or hug her for making me go. I do the latter, and we hug for a long time. I whisper thank you in her ear. We let go, and she smiles at me, truly smiles at me. We drive off toward our apartment and what I hope is a more promising future than I've allowed myself to think was possible before the grief retreat.

Epilogue

"Hi, boyfriend!" I'm waving like a crazy person across the quad like I haven't seen him in a month, but really we had coffee together this morning.

"Hi, girlfriend!" Ben acts just as happy to see me as I do him. He puts his arm around me, and we walk to his car together. We do this routine twice a week. We are THAT disgusting, lovey-dovey couple who can't keep their hands off of each other.

"How was class today?" I ask him.

"Thrilling as always. How was my favorite girl's class?" I love when he calls me that. It's amazing to be someone's number one person again.

"Perfect," I respond and kiss him on the cheek. I'm so happy to be back in school, but there is a little part of me that is angry at myself for not getting school right the first time around. I try to push the self-loathing part of me back down and remember that it wasn't my time back then. It's my time now though, and I'm soaking it all in. Ben and I scheduled some classes on the same days and time, so he could help keep me motivated to go to class; he's kind of like my college drop-out sponsor. It's sweet. I love being back at school and having goals so much, I don't really need a sponsor anymore, but I don't tell Ben that because I sort of love the school day routine with him.

Ben and I have been dating for about seven months. After I got home from the retreat, I noticed he hadn't given me his phone number or email address on the paper he wrote for me at our surprise party on the last night of the retreat.

His note just read, "I see your light trying to shine - let it." That one line confirmed that he was paying attention to me as he and the other counselors walked around during our narrative therapy. When I first read it, I was hopeful, but then the disappointment of not knowing how to contact him settled in. I was bummed for a while...until he showed up at Charlie's one day while I was working the afternoon shift. I was busy pouring drinks and didn't notice him at first, but then I felt someone staring at me. When I turned to see who it was and what they needed, I saw Ben sitting there with a goofy grin on his face. I wanted to play mad, but I was so happy to see him (and his dimples), I just couldn't fake anger. After that first day, he started showing up a few times a week, and we talked as much as we could between my drink pouring. On a Thursday night, he showed up with a bundle of blue hydrangeas as my shift was ending; he remembered that they're my favorite. Seven months later, he is still just as sweet and thoughtful as I thought he'd be.

"Have dinner with me, Silvia?" he asked.

Instead of saying yes and hugging him as he gave me the flowers, my stupid ass made a horrified face and said, "Now?" I only meant that I looked awful after work, but he looked like he thought I was rejecting him...

He gave me a weird look, and unsure of my meaning, started to pull his arm away that was trying to hand me the flowers.

"No! Yes. No. What I mean is no, don't take the flowers away, I want them and yes, let's have dinner." I smiled at him and took the flowers before he could change his mind. We headed out of Charlie's and toward our first of many dinners together.

Aside from my relationship with Ben, a lot of other things have changed in these last eight months since the grief retreat. Luci and Nick moved in together (yes, I know his name now, and we've actually been slowly bonding over the last several months). So it's just me now in the apartment. I would have been devastated by the separation from Luci if it wasn't for Ben and Jodie. I can't believe I'm saying this, but Jodie will be moving into Luci's old room for a few months until her new condo is ready. She is leaving the suburbs and moving into the city, near me, for a fresh start. I've been trying to help her tame the desire to please everyone and beg for their approval, and she's been helping me find other things to do besides drink. I started taking a photography class with her, and it's been really fun. I'm looking forward to having her here with me for a while.

I reached out to my parents recently. I just emailed them a couple lines to open the door. My new therapist (not Ben) is helping me learn to accept my parents for who they are. For all these years, I was feeling like I was the only one who lived through my sister's death. I didn't give my parents the latitude to grieve in their way, no matter how fucked up it was. I am learning to stop expecting things from them that they are not capable of giving to me. I'm getting there; it's a work in progress.

I stay in close touch with the rest of my new family. I have a standing dinner and drinks night with Thomas once a week (sometimes more); sometimes he brings his new boyfriend-who-isn't-his-boyfriend-but-kinda-is. I've gone to visit Tammy a few times. She lives a state away, but it's an easy, scenic drive. We walked her dogs together, and she took me to her and her mom's favorite Greek restaurant. I wish she lived closer, so I could see her more often. Diego lived the furthest away, and I never was able to visit him before he moved back to Mexico. He went back, so his mother can help him raise his two teenage daughters. The retreat helped him, but he didn't find the peace, or preview of peace to come, that the rest of us did; I hope he can find it back home with his family.

Ben has recently been helping me sort through all the crap in my apartment. I have boxes filled with Callie's old things and some of my mementos. The boxes are stacked in closets and my bedroom and even some in my living room. It's time to purge, but I find it so hard; I'm such a hoarder. Every time we sit down and go through a box, I'm only able to throw away one or two things. Ben's trying to help me believe that Callie won't be erased if I throw out some of her old things. We come to a box from my childhood bedroom, and he pulls out some small dolls caked with nail polish.

I grab them and yell, "Absolutely not! These stay." He laughs and pretends to take cover, like I'm going to smack him. I hold my dolls, and they feel so much lighter than they did in my child hands. I laugh to myself as I remember how the nail polish got on them and set the ruined doll family in the "Keep" pile. Ben pulls out a small box and opens it.

"Wow, these are really beautiful." He has found the matching necklaces from the road trip Callie and I took shortly before she died. I still hate saying "committed suicide." I mean, if someone dies from a heart attack, you say they died or passed away; you don't reference their cause of death every time you talk about them. I take the necklaces from him and hold them in my palm. My eyes begin to water, but I keep the tears in check. Ben squeezes my hand and gives me a grin; he knows the story behind the necklaces, and I can tell he isn't sure how I'll react to seeing them again.

"Seems a waste to keep them in a box," he says. He puts his arm around me and is speaking in a gentle tone that I know he uses for his patients. It annoys me a little, but I know he means well. He moves to put one of the necklaces on me, and I stop him.

"I can't. They were meant to be worn by sisters."

He continues to unclasp a necklace and puts it around my neck adjusting it, so it hangs at the longest setting.

Then he slides the second necklace around my neck and clasps it at its tightest setting, so that the necklaces are layered, and tells me, "Callie's in your heart. If you wear both, then sisters ARE wearing them." The tears come, but they aren't overwhelming; they are tears of nostalgia and don't last long. I stand and look in the mirror. I like how my necklace sits right at my collarbone, and Callie's hangs low, near my heart. A picture of Callie from prom night, standing behind me with her chin on my shoulder, flashes through my head. This feels right.